I0457702

IRRESISTIBLE:
A TERRAMATES NOVEL

LISA LACE

IRRESISTIBLE
Copyright © 2016 Toppings Publishing.
All rights reserved.

Disclaimer

This book is licensed for your personal enjoyment only.

Copyright Notes

No part of this publication may be used or reproduced in any form or by any means, including printing, photocopying, or otherwise, without written permission from the author, except in the case of brief quotations embodied in critical articles or review.

If you would like to use material from the book (other than just simply for reviewing the book), prior permission must be obtained by contacting the author at lisa@lisalace.com.

CONTENTS

CHAPTER 1 5
CHAPTER 2 14
CHAPTER 3 25
CHAPTER 4 36
CHAPTER 5 47
CHAPTER 6 55
CHAPTER 7 61
CHAPTER 8 70
CHAPTER 9 79
CHAPTER 10 88
CHAPTER 11 97
CHAPTER 12 106
CHAPTER 13 115
CHAPTER 14 125
CHAPTER 15 133
CHAPTER 16 146
CHAPTER 17 156
CHAPTER 18 166
CHAPTER 19 175
CHAPTER 20 182
CHAPTER 21 192
CHAPTER 22 202
CHAPTER 23 208
CHAPTER 24 218
CHAPTER 25 225
CHAPTER 26 231
CHAPTER 27 237
CHAPTER 28 ....**Error! Bookmark not defined.**
CHAPTER 29 ....**Error! Bookmark not defined.**
CHAPTER 30 ....**Error! Bookmark not defined.**

CHAPTER 31 .... Error! Bookmark not defined.
CHAPTER 32 .... Error! Bookmark not defined.
CHAPTER 33 .... Error! Bookmark not defined.
Other Books by Lisa Lace 243

CHAPTER 1

EMMY

"If you don't let me take your place on the flight, those men are going to kill me." I dropped my voice until it was barely above a whisper and focused on her light blue eyes. "Please."

My fear was a living thing, trembling through my bones and filling every space inside of me. I pressed my hands against my legs to keep them from shaking. If the stranger wouldn't cooperate, I was dead.

Everything Morley and I had worked for, and everything he had *died* for would go with me. One of the most precious cultural artifacts in the galaxy would go into the private collection of a selfish, self-centered, rich bastard who didn't give a shit that other people could also benefit from it.

I wouldn't let it happen. It was too important, and would help many people. I had to survive and find it. The woman in front of me looked conflicted.

"I don't even know who you are," she began.

"Look at this." I activated the computer on my forearm and tapped the communications unit until it displayed my bank account. I grabbed her arm. She frowned as I swiped her ID number. I created a pending transaction and pointed at my computer's display.

"500,000 credits, in your name. I'll transfer them now. It's a lot more than the cost of this spaceflight."

The woman gasped as she stared at the number.

"I'm in trouble. Please, do a girl a favor." I knew I was begging at this point, but they were coming this way, and it wouldn't be long before they spotted me.

I needed to get on the flight.

"Okay," she said, surprising me. "But you need to know something first."

I wasn't listening, though. I shook my head and had her speak her name into my computer, then I transferred the money into her account. I didn't think twice about it. Morley gave me the money for research.

I couldn't do any research if I were dead.

When it transferred, she allowed me to change the name on her ticket. "But listen," she said, more agitated than before. "You should know something first."

I shook my head. "I'm sorry, but I don't have the time. Thank you." I started moving away. She would never know the depths of my gratitude. I glanced back at Abel's henchmen, who miraculously still hadn't spotted me, and thanked my lucky stars again.

When I reached the desk, there wasn't even a line. They were announcing final boarding for spaceflight 46789 to planet Stalwart in Sector 91. I had no idea where Sector 91 was. I had never been good at Interplanetary Geography in school, and now I wished I had been a better student.

Did it matter? Right now, all I cared about was getting far away from Earth.

The woman behind the desk verified the ticket. I ducked into the walkway leading to the spacecraft, knowing I wouldn't feel safe until we took off.

* * *

An hour later, the shuttle was still on the ground, and I was wondering if my luck had finally run out. The captain had announced a flight delay just before our scheduled departure time. My heart started to beat fast. Why was taking so long? Was there a problem with the shuttle? I couldn't afford to have a delay, especially if it meant I would have to transfer to another ship.

Two men entered the spacecraft, and I ducked down into my seat. It was the men Abel sent after me.

Shit.

I didn't think. I unbuckled, got out of my seat, and headed toward the bathrooms as they began searching the front of the shuttle. My breathing was erratic, but I tried not to look unusual, keeping my face as neutral as possible.

When I finally reached the bathrooms, I realized they would check those too, and I would be trapped. Was there a place they wouldn't check? Yes. The carry-on storage. Every passenger on an interplanetary flight was allowed a single piece of luggage for the multi-day trip between worlds and they were all stored in compartments during take-off.

I shuffled farther back, moving to the location of the baggage compartments. The flight staff were at the front of the ship for the launch. No one was around.

I opened one of the large doors and crept inside. I moved the luggage one piece at a time, carefully replacing it behind me until I had made my way down to the back. There was a suitcase-sized hole for me, and I slid into it. My knees pressed against my chest. I pulled a smaller suitcase on top of me, trying not to hyperventilate in the small space.

As a final precaution, I swiped on my computer and activated a program to hide my body signature. I didn't know if they were using scanners, but I wasn't going to take a chance.

Then it was time to wait.

It seemed like I was trapped in that tiny, dark compartment forever, afraid to move and as still as a statue. But finally the door was wrenched open, and I heard men speaking as they peered in the cargo hold. They weren't speaking Standard, which was the language of the galaxy.

Years ago, most planets had adopted Standard as the primary language of trade and business. If the men weren't speaking Standard, it meant they didn't want anyone understanding what they were saying.

Fortunately, I knew the language they were speaking. It was English.

Despite the widespread use of Standard, a few of the old languages survived in pockets on every planet. Earth was no different. Many of its poorest and most technologically backward areas still spoke English. It was surely the spoken language in whatever district bred Abel.

Morley had been a stickler for being able to understand things for ourselves. He said that if we needed someone else to translate old documents and the writing on artifacts, we would never know if they were accurate. And what if we found a secret, and didn't want anyone else to know about what we had found?

He had made me learn English for our studies on Earth. He had learned the language twenty-five years earlier himself when he had been a graduate student in archeology, and I had still been in kindergarten. I had complained about the irregular tenses and ridiculous spellings. Standard had none of that. If there was a letter, it sounded like what it looked like, and nothing else. It was almost impossible to spell anything incorrectly because Standard was a created language.

Morley didn't care about my complaints. He had made me keep on with my lessons until I was fluent. I didn't speak it often, but I learned languages with ease, and people had mistaken me for a native speaker before.

As if learning English wasn't hard enough, later on, he also made me learn Karfalun. It was the ancient language of Heralla, a place where someone hid the Silver Mestolo of Zelia. And if I had thought English was difficult, I should have saved my breath to complain about the new language.

"She couldn't have gotten on this spaceship," one man said in English. "Our scanners would have found her. There's nothing but inanimate luggage in here. We should go back and do a thorough sweep of the spaceport."

"The boss will kill us if we let her get away. She's got the key to the latest old piece of junk he has his heart set on."

"Look, the compartment is full. She can't be in here. Let's go. The boss's pockets are deep, but not that deep. If the spaceport officials look closely at our papers, we'll be in trouble. It's time get out of here."

"Let's try one more time. You check this compartment, and I'll check the other one. Then we'll go."

I held my breath, but the man assigned to search my area didn't seem to be doing anything. I heard him shuffling things around at the front of the compartment at first, but then he started tapping on his computer as he waited for his partner.

"Did you find anything?"

"Nothing. She's not in here. Let's get off the shuttle before we get arrested for forging papers and delaying the flight."

There was no response, but soon the door closed, and I was in darkness again. I waited as long as I dared before trying to get out. I couldn't be in the luggage compartment when the shuttle took off, or I would have escaped one death only to find another.

I climbed back over the luggage to the door and peeked out. There didn't appear to be anyone around. I quickly emerged and shut the door, being as quiet as I could. I walked on soft feet to the bathroom, using it before returning to my seat. When I sat down, I heard an announcement to strap in for take-off.

I used two crisscrossing belts to secure myself. As soon as the sound of the shuttle taking off filled the spaceship, I knew I was leaving Earth, where I had grown up.

I let out a deep sigh. I was safe from Abel, for now.

* * *

Four days later, I stared at the viewscreen as the turquoise planet increased in size. Something had been on my mind now that my life wasn't in immediate danger.

What had that woman wanted to tell me? She seemed anxious and hadn't liked it when I brushed her off.

Now I felt like I should have listened to her. My gut told me that I had escaped one sticky situation and dove straight into another one. I just didn't know anything about the new problem.

Once we landed, I let everyone exit in front of me, stalling before I left the shuttle. I wasn't sure what was making me uneasy, but I had learned to trust my intuition. And my intuition was saying that there was nothing but trouble for me when I stepped off the spaceship.

I was slowly packing up my bags and starting to maneuver up the aisle when a man entered the spacecraft.

"There it is, sir," one of the attendants said, pointing at me. "Seat 257. Is this the person you're looking for?"

I lifted my eyes and saw a handsome alien man. His eyes were the deepest black. I felt that I might fall into them and never emerge if I wasn't careful. His hair was black as well. He had a light purple stripe that ran diagonally across one eye, ending at his nose. The net effect was to give him a rakish look as if he had a permanent black eye.

I caught my breath at the alien look of the male in front of me. I knew in my mind that we were all descended from the Great Race, but there were small differences between people of different planets. He also wore some of the most expensive clothes I had ever seen. The tight shirt showed off his well-defined chest, abs, and biceps. He was wearing pants that looked as though they had been tailor-made for him — and maybe they had been.

I noticed his lips were strong-looking but thin. He had an air of authority, though it didn't go with his fancy clothes. And I spotted a chain around his neck.

All of these thoughts passed through my mind in a few seconds as I stared into the stranger's eyes. He blinked, surprised when he saw my face. I froze. I wasn't cretain what was going on but he knew I wasn't the woman who was supposed to be on this spaceflight. I held my breath, waiting to see if he would say anything.

"Sir?" she asked again. "Is it her?"

He only hesitated a moment. "Yes, she's the one."

What did he mean?

He didn't say anything else. I smiled at the attendant and began walking up the aisle. As the man turned, I followed him off the shuttle, wondering what I had gotten myself into this time.

CHAPTER 2

VEN

Pandenn was late again.

He was always late. He had been late when we were in basic training together, and he had been late when we served in the same unit. He was even late for his first son's birth. People joked that when the grim reaper came, he would be late for that appointment too.

It didn't matter. I had nothing but time to kill. He could be five, ten, or twenty-six minutes late, and it wouldn't matter to me. I had nothing better to do. I had retired from the military and was independently wealthy. There was nowhere I needed to be.

My uncle had left me an enormous fortune that paid for my lifestyle. The amount of money I had was, frankly, ridiculous.

On some planets, I wouldn't be old enough to retire yet, but in the Stalwart military, you're free to go after you turn twenty-five years old. It's even easier if you have a lot of medals, like me.

I had needed to retire. I couldn't take it anymore. I had risked my life time and time again to accomplish the mission and save people. It had been worth it at the time, and I might do it all over again if I had to, just to make sure my friends came back alive.

But I was sick of never knowing whether I would see the next morning. I was sick of active combat. I was sick of taking over weaker planets. I was sick of it all. Somehow I had lost my passion for fighting.

There was a time when I had believed fully in what I was doing. We brought a better government and a better life to the planets with whom we 'entered into economic partnerships'. That's what our government called it.

From another point of view, we entered planets covertly, seized the centers of power and threatened to annihilate them if they didn't do everything we ordered. The further up the ranks I got, the more clearly I saw what we were doing.

I hated it.

So I left. I retired two years ago and I had never missed the service. I didn't need to work, and I had a beautiful house. Servants took care of everything. I had the nicest clothes and ate at the best restaurants. I worked out, read extensively, and continued training in various martial arts to keep my reflexes sharp.

I had everything, but I was bored.

The first year was excellent. I had been tired and burned out. I took a year to relax and lie on the beach. I rested and enjoyed the good life.

But by the beginning of the second year, everything was starting to wear thin. Things were *too* perfect. The people who worked for me never said anything I disliked.

My friends never had time to do anything because they were still working and had real lives.

Now I was at the start of my third year of retirement. I was sure I was going to lose my mind. I needed something to do, but I didn't know what. All my ideas seemed stupid. I was at my wits' end. It almost made me want to go back to the military.

Almost. But not quite.

"Hi, Ven." Pandenn sat down like nothing was the matter. He was a half hour later than our scheduled time. I looked up at him, shaking my head. The light purple stripes spread in a random fashion across the skin of anyone from Stalwart were dark on his face. He must have been running to get here. The rest of his face was red from exertion.

"How are Jalla and the kids?"

"Awesome. How are you?"

He held his fist out, and we bumped the sides of our hands together to greet each other. He dressed like a hobo, as usual — ripped pants and a dirty looking shirt that had seen better days. I was sure that when we went out for lunch together, people thought I had picked up a beggar off the streets and was being kind enough to buy him lunch.

I always bought. Pandenn had more than enough money to pay, but he was too cheap. I always offered to pay. What else did I have to do with all my money?

"Do you want the polite answer?" I leaned back. "Or the truthful one?"

"Truthful, always. It's usually more interesting than the other option." He lifted an eyebrow. "Did that chick you were dating agree to take it in the ass?"

"No." I shook my head, then amended my statement. "Well, yes, she did, but we're not together anymore."

His jaw dropped. "She did?"

"Yes, but we're talking about me right now, not her."

"Was it good?"

"Mind-blowing. Will you listen to me?"

"How long did she last? Two weeks?" His eyes stared up and to the right, trying to remember.

"Eleven days."

"She was hot," he said, still off in his own world. "That must have been some incredible sex."

"Will you listen, for fuck's sake, Pan?"

He looked startled when I swore and focused on my face. "What?"

"I don't want to talk about her." I forced myself to swallow the impatience with my old friend. He had always like been this. Why did I expect him to be different today?

17

"Oh." He looked taken aback. "What do you want to talk about then?"

"You asked me how I was, and you said you wanted a truthful answer."

"Right. So...How are you?"

"The truth?" I said, knowing I had his attention now. He nodded. "I'm..." I hesitated.

"What?"

"I don't want to tell you," I confessed. "It's going to sound ungrateful...like I don't appreciate what I have."

"Just tell me. Come on. Lay it on me. I can take it," he said, making a come-hither motion with both hands.

I smiled. Good old Pandenn. I could count on him to understand. I knew that. "I'm bored."

The server came at that moment and took his drink order. "Well, that's not what I was expecting."

"I know. It sounds stupid. I have more than enough money. A lovely house. People who take care of my every need…"

"…hot women who are willing to do just about anything in your bed. I cannot *believe* she agreed to that position," he said, getting a far-off look in his eyes again. "Why don't you get a job? You're too young to be retired."

"I thought of that, but I'm not sure what I would do. Nothing seems right."

"Pretend I'm a shrink. Tell me exactly how you feel and I'll fix you up."

Pandenn had done his minor in psychology, and he considered himself an amateur psychologist. I sighed. The server returned and placed a purple drink in front of Pan.

"I'm not interested in anything. I get bored with my books and my training lately. And..."

"And?" He was always interested in what was typically left unsaid.

"I guess I wish I had someone to hang around with at home, in the evening, instead of going out with friends. Not like you coming over and playing holographic games. Just...oh, I don't know..."

He thought for a moment and gazed at me appraisingly. "I know what you need. You need a proper woman. A wife!"

"What?" I started laughing.

"Jalla is the best thing that ever happened to me."

"But you dated her. You love her. I don't have anyone like that."

"Sometimes you have to get married anyway." He had a smirk on his face.

I made a dismissive gesture. "You're just fucking with me. You want to order anything or are you only having a drink?" I picked up my menu. I didn't know why I tried to talk about meaningful things with Pandenn. He just wasn't the serious type.

"No." He put out his hand, and the tone of his voice made me look up. "I mean it."

"Pan, shut up. I'm not going to walk up to a stranger and say, "Hey there, sweetie. You look fine. Let's get married.""

"I'm not talking about any stranger. Have you considered a mail-order bride?"

I stared at him, not bothering to say anything. This guy had lost it. "What are you talking about?"

"Jal and I just watched a documentary on a company from Earth called TerraMates. They're very reputable. They monitor everything to make sure both parties are satisfied with the arrangement. You can get divorced after a year if things aren't working."

"Are you shitting me?"

"I'm not. I swear," he said, holding up his hands. "Call Jalla right now. She'll back me up."

I shook my head. "You're crazy. I'm not getting a mail order bride."

"Look, consider it, Ven. You've never been good at dating or choosing your women. Why not give someone else a shot? If you want company or someone to be there for you, there's nothing like a wife."

"You're saying that because you have a wife that loves you, buddy. I'm sure there's a big difference between Jalla and a mail-order bride."

"Here's the thing," he said, leaning in. "It's hard to believe, but if they're telling the truth, they say that only two percent of their marriages end in divorce."

I looked at him skeptically. "It sounds impossible."

"You'll never know until you try it, Ven. You can grow to love someone."

I frowned, shaking my head.

"Don't be stupid, Ven." I felt my temper flare at his innocent use of the word stupid. I couldn't stand being called dumb. "Let TerraMates take care of your bride. If you don't like her, divorce her after a year."

He leaned back and smiled. I stared at him blankly.

"Arranged marriages are a time-honored tradition on many planets, you know," he said, folding his arms over his chest as if that clinched his argument.

"You're nuts," I repeated. "Are we going to order something? We're supposed to be eating lunch. By the time I get my food, it's going to be time for dinner."

He laughed. "You can make fun of it all you want, Ven, but I'm sending you the link to the documentary. You can watch it while you sit at home by yourself tonight."

"Bastard," I said, trying to look at the menu.

"You're right. I am a bastard." He tapped the computer unit on his forearm.

A moment later, my arm lit up with his message and I looked into his eyes. "I'm never going to marry a stranger from some mail-order bride agency, Pandenn."

He grinned at me. "Never say never."

* * *

I walked into my den and looked around at my belongings. I liked things to be neat. It dated back to my time in the military — a desire for tidiness, which bordered on obsession. Usually, the staff kept everything in perfect order. But once in a while, I would find that someone had left a task undone or been a little sloppy. I didn't blame them. It wasn't their house. But I noticed everything.

Today, for instance, I saw when I walked through the door that the housekeeper had dusted and bumped my favorite painting. It wasn't straight anymore. I couldn't stand having a crooked picture frame. I walked over and adjusted the image. There. Perfectly straight...no. I shifted it back the other way. After a minute of adjusting, I was satisfied.

Since I didn't have anything else to do that evening, I watched the documentary. I wasn't interested, of course, but I was alone and bored. All the staff was gone home or to their apartments.

I watched as a happy couple on a sailing ship told their story. I rolled my eyes. Why were they on a sailing ship? We had fucking space travel. They hadn't meant to stay married and had only gone to TerraMates for personal reasons. She had needed the money to pay for her brother's gambling debts, and he had needed a wife to stay out of jail. In the end, they stayed married because they had fallen in love.

There was story after story about happy couples. For a minute, I was convinced that some people could find love that way. But I wasn't the kind of guy who would sign up and have someone else pick my wife for me. Besides, when I looked them up, the man had to pay an exorbitantly high fee. They went through your life with a fine-toothed comb. I could afford the credits, and I certainly didn't have anything to hide…but I liked my privacy. I didn't want anyone poking around in my business.

I turned off the documentary and stood up. It was time for bed. I looked around at the empty room in the lonely, echoing house.

Hollow. That was exactly the word to describe it.

Maybe Pan was right. Maybe I *did* need a woman for more than eleven days. I had to admit it would be nice.

But I couldn't think of a single woman who I would ever consider marrying.

Even if I did need a wife, I wasn't going to let anyone else pick the woman for me. I was in charge.

CHAPTER 3

VEN

I wasn't in charge of anything.

The sobering thought occurred to me as I sat in my lawyer's office, listening to him telling me I had to get married. I realized I needed to use TerraMates after all. After my postulating and swearing up and down that I would never have a mail-order bride, I was going to have them ship one out to me.

Fuck. Pan was going to make fun of me forever.

I didn't want to have to resort to these measures, but I didn't see any way out of it. Without a wife, I was going to lose everything.

It started when my uncle's representatives called me and asked to speak with my wife. I didn't have one. The snarky lawyer explained that if I didn't have a wife by the time I turned thirty, my inheritance, Uncle Mastoh's entire fortune, would be given to charity.

I knew I wouldn't gain control over all the money until I was thirty. I had been living off the interest from the investments. I vaguely remembered hearing something about having to get married. But I had been young and hung over during the reading of the will. Thirty had seemed like a long way away. Before I left the military, I banked all the interest. I didn't start spending it until I retired.

I needed a wife to keep the money. It couldn't be that onerous. And didn't I want to be married in the abstract, theoretical sense? The inheritance was giving me a push in the right direction. More like a shove, I suppose. I could always take the divorce at the end of the year, and I would be able to keep my standard of living.

I winced, as I realized how shallow my thoughts were. I consoled myself with a single thought. By hanging on to my uncle's money, I was fulfilling the vow I made to myself as a teenager in my family's small, dingy apartment. At the time, I swore I would get out of that life, earn money, and become wealthy. I would never treat my family like my father had, taking us close to homelessness multiple times.

I wasn't going to let my uncle's money go. I needed it for my future children. They would have everything they needed, and they would never live a life like mine.

Everything would work out in the end. Pandenn would say it was the universe working in mysterious ways. But he would never find out about my decision or that he was right about TerraMates.

I needed to start now before I lost my courage. I pulled up the documentary again and started the application process.

* * *

Two weeks later, I had jumped through all the hoops, gone through the interviews, paid the ridiculously high fees, and received a birth control shot, which lasted a year. I was ready to find a mate.

I swung back and forth on my porch swing, feeling impatient. When one of my servants approached me, I felt a twinge of apprehension. I had asked to be left alone for the rest of the day unless it was important. What could be so important that he would disturb me?

"Sir?" Elon looked nervous. "I know you said not to..."

"Disturb me unless it was important," I finished for him. "I know. Well, you've disturbed me. What is it?"

"A package came for you. I thought you were waiting for it."

He held out a small square box that I recognized immediately as an old-fashioned hologram message. There were far more sophisticated technologies available, but TerraMates was an Earth-based company. Even though they had plenty of lovely human woman dying to get off their backward little world, they lacked many of the refinements possessed by civilized planets, such as up-to-date messaging technology.

I thanked Elon and held the box in my hand. It had been a long time since I had felt this nervous. I was a decorated war veteran who had risked his life many times in the military. I had no reason to fear this trinket.

I activated it, and a full-sized hologram appeared. Not everyone went to the trouble of setting up a hologram profile. In fact, this was the first out of ten I had seen. I placed the box on the floor and stepped back to look at her assets. There was only one word for the image of the woman in front of me, and that was...

Wow.

I sat back on the swing, pushing the ground with my feet to get it rocking again.

She was tall, with long shining blonde hair that hung to her ass. Her eyes were pale blue, a rare color on my planet. Her body was thin and her skin was pale. As she turned to me, I could see that her legs were just the way I liked them — long and thin, perfect for wrapping around my waist.

TerraMates had matched the physical profile I requested. I wondered about her personality.

"Hi, Montana."

"Hello, there, Ven." Her voice was sultry. Could this woman be any more perfect?

"What do you do for a living, Montana?" I asked, rocking a little faster in the swing.

"I'm a systems analyst. I have two years of college training and a certification."

Good. She was smart, but not too smart.

Anyone could be a systems analyst. It might seem insecure, but I didn't like brilliant women. They intimidated me. I didn't like them stupid, either. Don't get me wrong. I wasn't into bimbos. But middle-of-the-road was just right.

"You sound smart. What do you like to do in your spare time?"

"Well, Ven, I enjoy dancing and horseback riding."

Horseback riding? What the hell was that?

"Oh, that's interesting."

That was enough talking to a hologram for me. I leaned over and slapped the box, turning it off. I reclined on the swing and steepled my fingers, smiling to myself. She was the woman. The woman I was going to spend the rest of my life with — or at the very least, the next year. They had matched me with the perfect woman.

I couldn't wait to meet her.

* * *

On the day Montana was supposed to arrive at the space station, I arrived an hour early. I thought I might have looked too eager, but I couldn't wait to meet her. We were going to be perfect for each other. Thank goodness her flight had arrived on time. It was going to be down to the wire, but as long as we got married today, it would be okay. Everything would work out with Uncle Mastoh's will.

I tapped my foot, thinking about Montana Willoughby, soon to be Montana Dofalar if she took my name. I pictured us going out dancing. Maybe she would show me some holograms of horseback riding, whatever that was.

And I definitely had some sexual fantasies featuring the leggy blonde. I couldn't wait to meet my fiancé and make her my wife. Everything was going to be different.

I wouldn't have an empty feeling inside anymore. I would have someone with whom I could spend time. Not only would she be around for me, but I could also keep my way of life and everything that had become important over the past three years.

I strolled back and forth in the spaceport, ignoring the other travelers. Finally, they announced her flight. I waited patiently as each person came off the ship, went through the scanners, and emerged from security.

I scanned each face to see if it was her. The last stragglers appeared, but none of them was Montana.

"Excuse me, aren't there any more passengers on board?"

The attendant frowned. "I'm not sure. Who are you looking for?"

"A human named Montana Willoughby. She's tall, with blonde hair and blue eyes."

The woman checked her console. "None of the ticket holders have that name," she said. "Is it possible she goes by something else?"

I shrugged. "I don't know. I've never met her." It felt weird to have to say that I was meeting someone I had never met, though I suppose spaceport employees heard these kinds of stories all the time. The attendant couldn't care less.

"I'll check for you." She disappeared through the gate. Five minutes later, I saw her again.

"There's only one woman left. She's taking a while to get packed up. Come and see if she's the one you're looking for."

I followed the attendant onto the shuttle. Something didn't feel right. If there was one thing I had learned in the military, it was that following my gut was the best policy. I touched a blaster which I always carried in my pocket. It was small but got the job done.

When I walked onto the shuttle, my eyebrows drew together as I caught sight of the only woman remaining on the ship. She wasn't Montana. I could tell right away.

She was small, with a sturdy frame that looked like she would be good at physical tasks, like climbing or carrying

31

cargo. Her figure was shapely, with full round breasts and hips that encouraged men to rest their hands on her side when they danced...if you liked that sort of a woman. She appeared to be busy packing up her bag. Why had she taken everything out of it? My uneasy feeling intensified.

Then she turned around, and I saw her eyes.

The moment our eyes met, I thought something drew all the air from my lungs. I couldn't get a breath. And my stomach felt peculiar. I found myself staring into her mesmerizing brown eyes.

I felt like the whole universe had just tilted and nothing was ever going to be the same again.

"Sir?" the attendant said, and I knew from the way she said it, she had already spoken to me before. "Is she the one?"

I waited only a moment more before speaking the words I knew would change my life.

"Yes, she's the one."

The woman looked troubled but didn't say anything. She played along, following me off the shuttle without saying a word.

I didn't know who she was. I didn't know why she was here instead of Montana. All I knew was that she was the one.

Whatever that meant.

* * *

"Wait, wait, wait." We stood on the outskirts of the arrival area. I was explaining my behavior for the fourth time. The first couple times didn't seem to be effective. "Are you telling me you want to marry me?"

"Yes," I said. "I mean, no. The woman whose ticket you came her on...she was supposed to marry me." I felt myself beginning to blush. Again. "She was my mail-order bride."

"Are you kidding me?" Emmy said, looking incredulous. "Nobody does that anymore."

"I'm completely serious. If you're willing, I don't care that you're not Montana. I'll marry you. I need to marry someone today."

She wasn't going to fall into my arms after that enticing proposition.

"I don't even know your name." She looked amazed that I would dare to suggest such a thing.

"It's Ven. If you don't want to, I don't blame you, but why were you on the shuttle in the first place? I needed to marry her today."

She couldn't stop looking at something or someone over my shoulder. Emmy started repositioning herself. She tried to play it cool, but I could tell she was putting me between her body and whoever she wanted to avoid.

"Never mind." Emmy smiled brightly, but an element of authenticity was missing. Something about it seemed fake. "I'll..."

She swallowed hard.

"I'll marry you. We better go now if you're in such a hurry. Come on."

She grabbed my arm, making sure to conceal herself behind my body. Soon we were quickly marching toward the exit.

A couple of men who looked like thugs brushed past us. I felt Emmy's hand on my arm get tense as we passed them. I got a good look at them and made a mental note of their appearance. I wasn't going to find out everything at the spaceport, but it might be useful to remember their appearance.

As we walked, I tried to organize my thoughts and accept reality. I wasn't going to get married to Montana, my self-selected perfect match. But Emmy had stepped up. I needed to get married, and that was the only thing that mattered. Everything else would sort itself out later.

A justice of the peace waited at the courthouse for us. We could do the deed within the next hour. After we had our certificates, we'd head straight to the lawyers and then home.

She could tell me her story, and I could tell her mine. We could spend the rest of the year together, and maybe even the rest of our lives.

A realization struck fear into my heart. I didn't know anything about Emmy.

Then I thought about what I would lose if I didn't marry her. The idea was appalling. I wouldn't go back to living the way I had as a child — poor and desperate. I had made a promise to myself to live a different lifestyle.

All I need to do was go the courthouse with a stranger and swear to love, honor, and protect her for the rest of my life.

CHAPTER 4

EMMY

I sat in the den of Ven's enormous mansion and tried to convince myself I was safe, at least temporarily. I didn't want to think about the fact that I had just married a complete stranger. An alien. My hands started to shake.

I hadn't planned on getting married, ever. My mother raised me by herself. As soon as I got my scholarship for archeology at the university, I left for school and never looked back.

Even though I went to my house for Christmas every year, it never seemed like home ever again. Once Morley took me on as an assistant, we traveled all over the galaxy.

Some people called us treasure hunters, but I considered the term derogatory. Like calling a freedom fighter a terrorist. Morely was the real deal among archeologists. He and I had found the Golden Chalice of Rilagoon's fourth King on Dorset.

After our adventure, I went back to school to complete my master's degree and Ph.D., taking only three years to complete them both. I was the youngest person in two hundred years to achieve a Ph.D. in my field.

I thought of myself as one of the best in school, and the university was no different. I like thinking and figuring things out. That's one of the reasons I became an archeologist in the first place. The other reasons were getting out of my dead-end city and making something better of myself.

Mom was a terrific person, but she never wanted to be anything more than a receptionist. I didn't have a problem with that, but I wanted more for myself. Marriage had never entered into the equation. I didn't need or want a man. My mom had managed without one and I would too.

I had a little fling with Christopher during my second year of grad school. It only lasted four days and the first two days were the best part of the whole thing. We never had sex, which was the crux of the problem in our relationship. I didn't regret my decision. He was a loser, anyway.

I could take care of my desires by myself, thank you very much. I certainly didn't want some oaf sticking his big cock up inside me, thrusting a couple of times, and then collapsing for the night. That wasn't my idea of a good time. I didn't understand what the big deal was. Why was everyone always making such a fuss about sex? It seemed like a waste of time.

A great view of the planet Stalwart was right out the window. Mountains covered most of the surface. I had read about my destination in a little brochure on the spaceflight. The planet was known for a formidable military and economic prosperity.

I wasn't sure if I would return to this world after finding the silver ladle, but if I ever came back, I hoped to do some rock climbing. I loved the exercise and was accustomed to getting away almost every other weekend at home.

Ven chose that moment to walk back in the room. When I twisted my head to look at him, a shiver went through my body. He was definitely hot and incredibly sexy, but I had made up my mind about fucking. I wasn't going to change it.

The thought of sex and Ven reminded me that we were married. Was I *supposed* to fuck him? I recoiled at the idea of sleeping with a stranger and wondered if he would try to force himself on me.

The operative word being try. I had been training in martial arts since I was young. I had practiced karate and some tai kwon do. I had also spent time fooling around with judo for fun. I was small, but I knew how to take care of myself.

I eyed him warily as one of his servants put an interesting-looking pink drink in front of me. If he tried to force me to fuck him, I would take him out.

He smiled at me. I would be polite as long as he kept his hands out of my pants.

"So." He sat down in the chair across from me. His house was enormous and looked like an interior designer had gone to town. Ven seemed to have plenty of credits to burn. I had expected he was wealthy when I noticed his clothing at the spaceport, but this was another level of opulence.

"So," I repeated, wondering if I should drink the pink concoction in front of me.

"I think we should both tell our stories from the beginning. We need to understand each other a lot better than we do now."

"Okay," I agreed. "As long as you go first."

He looked put out. I guessed he didn't want me giving orders. I didn't retract my statement, however. I simply waited for him to start talking. If he didn't like who I was, he could divorce me. I didn't need to be married to him. Ven needed me as a wife.

"I hadn't planned on getting married. It turned out that there was an obscure clause in my uncle's will. He left me a lot of credits, and his legacy paid for this house and everything else."

There was more? I wondered what everything else meant.

"I've made some investments with the money. I bought this house and some toys. There are a lot of bills. If I lost that money, I would have to do the unthinkable." He paused and seemed unsure of what to say next.

"What's unthinkable? Do you mean live like an average person, or get a job? Declare bankruptcy?"

"Maybe all of the above. I haven't always lived like this, but I've become accustomed to the lifestyle. My friend suggested a mail-order bride company, which seemed like the perfect way to have everything I wanted. Things would stay the same."

It seemed ridiculous to me that someone could be so attached to being rich.

"And I would find someone to keep me company."

"Most people can do that without hired help," I murmured.

He looked mildly annoyed with me. "Then everything would be okay. My life wouldn't have to change."

"Do you know what that sounds like to me?" I asked. "Boring."

He gazed at me. I didn't know if he was confused or irritated. He didn't go on with his tale of woe immediately, but continued to stare at me like I was the newest exhibit at the zoo and he had never seen anything like me before.

"How could you know I was bored? When I talk about my life, most people think it's amazing. You just met me. How could you know it's tedious?"

I shrugged and picked up a glass filled with pink liquid. "What is this?"

"Gorjill juice."

"Is it poisonous?" Ven glanced at me sharply, then decided I was joking and laughed nervously.

"I'm not trying to kill you. It's delicious. I wouldn't poison you." He looked at me earnestly.

"No, of course not. If you wanted to kill me, you would do it with the gun in your pocket." I took a tentative sip of the drink. The sweet liquid rolled across my tongue, and I closed my eyes in bliss. "It tastes wonderful." I took a larger swallow, closing my eyes to savor the taste. When I opened my eyes, he was looking at me again.

"I have two questions for you," he said, holding up his index finger. "One. How did you know it would be boring? You still haven't answered me."

"I don't know," I said. "Sitting around all day in a big house that has no personality, without any meaningful work and no one to spend time with? It sounds boring to me."

He didn't say anything as he digested my comment.

"What's the other question?" I looked at the glass and felt sad the incredible drink was almost gone.

"How did you know I had a gun in my pocket?"

"Cultural anthropology. I did a comparative study for one of my classes. It was on weapons of the present and past. It's a hobby of mine."

He stared at me suspiciously.

"There's a giant gun-shaped bulge in your pants. It's impossible to miss."

"Weapons are a hobby of yours?" He seemed mystified. I wondered what sort of woman he had expected. I couldn't help grinning mischievously when I thought of the boring, perfect-looking tall, thin, blonde woman I traded places with. I might not be a classical beauty, but I could guarantee I wouldn't be boring.

I nodded. "The shape was obvious when we hailing the car at the spaceport. What kind of guy is carrying when he goes to pick up his fiancé?" I asked, mostly to myself.

"I have another question for you."

"Shoot." I laughed. "Not literally, please. I mean, go ahead."

He looked puzzled again and spoke with only a trace of embarrassment.

"There's a term my fiancé used that I didn't understand, and I couldn't find references to it anywhere. It's been bothering me. What is a horseback?"

It was my turn to be confused.

"A horseback? You mean, the back of a horse?"

"No, riding a horseback."

"That's not a thing." I shook my head and swallowed the last of my drink.

"It's not? She specifically said she enjoyed horseback riding."

"I see. There's a language problem." I finally understood what he meant. "She's referring to an animal from Earth. A horse is a mammal with four legs, and it's pretty fast. It's almost extinct now, but they used to be quite common. Some people might still ride them."

"I guess so. It seemed like a weird thing to want to do."

"You didn't finish your story. You were bored, and you didn't want anything to change," I prompted.

He was definitely irritated now and he wasn't trying to hide it any longer.

"The will says that I have to get married by the time I turn thirty or all the money goes to charity. I'm sure they said something about this at the reading of the will, but I didn't pay attention to it at the time. I assumed I'd be married by now."

"You decided to order up a bride to solve your problem? That's surprising. You don't seem like the type to do something like that."

"I don't?"

"You're good looking, and you're rich. If I had to guess, I would think you could easily find someone to sacrifice and a live a luxurious lifestyle in a big house where they didn't have to work."

"There were other factors to consider."

"What kind of other factors?"

He didn't elaborate. "I contacted TerraMates. They set everything up so Montana would come here to get married. Of course, she didn't come, and I was fortunate to marry you instead."

The words sent an electric feeling rushing through my body as he stared at me. I felt like I should say something.

"You're crazy. And I'm crazy too for marrying you."

"Maybe, but there were reasons behind my actions. Come to think of it, there were probably reasons behind your actions too. Who were those men at the spaceport?" he asked innocently.

I was shocked at his audacity, and I didn't have a ready response. "You aren't the only one with a perceptive eye," he said.

"Apparently not." I was impressed in spite of myself.

"What's your story? I'm going to think you're lying to me if you take much longer."

I hesitated, wondering how much I could safely tell him. I didn't know him at all, and I didn't feel comfortable sharing too much, but I couldn't stay in his big house for much longer. I had to find the artifact or all of my efforts would have been in vain. Morley's death would be a useless sacrifice.

I made a split-second decision to only tell my husband part of the truth. Just enough to get me out of here. I needed to get to the artifact before Abel did, but what if Ven went to the police and revealed everything in a misguided attempt to do the right thing? I had no confidence the authorities would be able to stop Abel. They had never been successful before. I was certain that if he beat me to the artifact, he wouldn't let me go on my merry way either, considering what I knew about his involvement.

Once the ladle was secure, I could tell Ven everything. Until then, I would have to keep my secrets to myself. It occurred to me that a man with a big bankroll could easily fund a trip to Heralla. I smiled to myself.

"They were pursuing me against my will."

"Why?"

I hesitated again. "I'd rather not say. I can tell you eventually but for now, it's best for me to keep some things private." He frowned, and I knew I had said the wrong thing. "I promise what I tell you will be the truth. I might not be able to say everything. That's going to have to do for now."

I thought I detected a grudging acceptance in his expression.

"I know this can't be easy for you," he said, staring down at his hands. "I expected to marry a stranger today, even if it wasn't you. You were thrown into this marriage. But I swore to protect you, and I can't do that if I don't know why you're scared of them."

He raised his big black eyes to meet mine. The purple diagonal stripe across his left eye made him look even more handsome than before. My heart beat faster, and I couldn't look away from his gaze. I knew I had to give him something.

I hesitated, then shrugged. I might as well say it all at once. "They want to kidnap me, and probably kill me."

CHAPTER 5

VEN

I lay in bed alone on my wedding night. In the distance, I could hear night birds calling, and they sounded lonely. I heard a creak from the room where Emmy was staying. She was probably rolling over in her sleep. I briefly wondered what she was wearing but stopped immediately. Thinking about Emmy in bed wasn't going to get me anywhere.

I flipped onto my stomach, pulling the covers with me and allowing my leg to stick out. I punched the pillow a few times and laid my head back down, trying to get comfortable.

It wasn't supposed to be like this.

I had imagined Montana and I would hit it off right away. We would have an instant connection and chemistry because we matched perfectly. I thought we could get married and have a romantic dinner. Then I would take her to bed. She would wrap her long legs around my butt, and I would fuck her until we both came.

Perhaps it was a little childish, but I couldn't help my feelings. I was angry and upset that things had turned out differently. I tried to remind myself that it didn't matter who came out of the spaceship. I needed a wife. Now I had one. Emmy wasn't everything I had expected, but she was good enough.

My brain tried to give myself a message, but my heart didn't want to listen to it. The reality was that I wanted more from my wife. I hoped for someone who would have the slightest interest in me. Emmy was most concerned with keeping secrets. She claimed she had a good reason for not telling me things, but I didn't believe her.

After we had told our stories, she looked nervous about our first night together. I explained that one of the stipulations in the TerraMates contract was any sex had to be consensual. That bit of happy news brightened her immediately, which made me feel like an asshole. Had she been worried about fucking me? Would that have been such a terrible thing? Or did I look like a rapist?

She was insulting my manhood, but I couldn't say anything about it. My pride would have to hurt privately.

Suddenly I couldn't stop thinking about the things about her that irritated me. I remembered how she had noticed a gun in my pocket. If a human woman from Earth could see it, I realized anyone could, and I would need a smaller firearm.

I wondered why the men wanted to kill her. She seemed intelligent, but not dangerous. I had always felt intimidated by smart women. Emmy made me uncomfortable.

Why didn't she have any luggage, and why did she take Montana's ticket?

I wasn't going to get answers anytime soon, especially if we were in different rooms. Emmy said she couldn't tell me. I knew the reason why. She didn't trust me. She didn't know anything about me and knew nothing about my character. She had no reason to have faith in me.

Still, the sheer number of questions was annoying.

I wanted her to look up to me, rely on me, and trust me implicitly. I was sure that was what Montana would have done.

What I didn't want was a woman who looked at me like she was my equal. She was a human. I didn't want one who could stand on her own two feet and refused to trust me. Emmy seemed too capable of defending herself.

Wasn't a wife suppose to be dependent on her husband? And what kind of woman had a hobby that involved weapons?

I had never imagined a female like this could exist.

Emmy was only one room over. When I told her we didn't have to sleep together, she let out a sigh of relief, and I knew what that meant. I immediately led her to the guest bedroom adjacent to my room.

After we arrived at my house, I asked for her size. My housekeeper went out and purchased a closet full of clothes to fit her. She was amazed to find clean pajamas ready for her on the bed. It was perfect for her, but I felt incomplete when I bid her goodnight and went to bed alone.

What a terrible wedding night. I felt let down. I expected more from my marriage, arranged or not.

That was before Emmy came into the picture and messed everything up. I felt my heart hardening at the thought of my new wife.

We wouldn't have to spend too much time together. In the shower, I had decided it was time for me to start working again. If the marriage didn't work out, I would have to find something else to give my life meaning.

Work was the next best thing to a happy marriage. Emmy might be beautiful and intelligent, but she would never be a wife like Montana.

My dream of a happy marriage was over.

* * *

EMMY

I wondered what Ven was doing over in his room by himself. I hoped he was sleeping and not imagining me naked. I shook my head and went back to assessing the climbing equipment I borrowed from the front closet.

Since I didn't have access to a shop, the climbing gear I gathered in a little detour after I went to the bathroom would have to do. Thank goodness I happened to have a large carabiner on me. It was big enough to reach around one of the poles of the canopy bed in my room. It attached tightly with a sharp click. I yanked the rope, and it seemed to hold, so I took the remaining line and dropped it out the window.

I was capable of using the front door like a normal person, but I had reservations about it. There was a sophisticated alarm system attached to the house. Although Ven had keyed my biometric signature into the security system, if I walked out the front door he would know too much information about me. He would be able to determine exactly when I left and maybe even the direction I headed.

My plan was to climb out the window instead. In the morning, when he found the rope, it would be obvious how I escaped. By then I would be on the next spaceship to Heralla and out of his hair.

He said he needed a wife. Now he had one. He could keep his fortune. The only thing I would take was some climbing equipment and 500,000 credits from our joint bank account.

I wondered if he would notice the missing money. The number of credits was nothing to someone with his wealth. It was the same amount I gave to his fiancee. I would be getting back the money that was supposed to fund the rest of the expedition to get the ladle. I needed the money for space travel. I didn't think Ven would begrudge me a few credits as long as I helped him keep the rest of them.

But I still didn't ask him about it.

I felt mildly guilty about leaving in the middle of the night without saying goodbye. Ven seemed like a good man, but I had an agenda. Getting married and playing house wasn't a part of it.

I lowered myself out the window and climbed down the rope. I didn't bother with a harness because I was only descending three floors. If I couldn't go down three floors without falling, I deserved to die. There were a few dangerous-looking rocks at the bottom, but everything was rocky on this planet.

I had faith in my arms. I possessed plenty of upper body strength, and I had always been good at rope climbing. In school, I would quickly go all the way up to the ceiling of the gym on the climbing ropes and hang at the top for a while before coming back down.

My life was spent taking risks, not like Ven. I imagined him sleeping contentedly in his bed, not wanting anything in his dull luxurious life to ever change. Part of me pitied him. He was attached to material possessions and his lifestyle. I could see that a spark had left him a long time ago.

I imagined he might have been more fun earlier in his life, before he became a stick-in-the-mud. For a moment, I wondered what would happen if I stayed around long enough to help him remember who he could be. But I shut down the thought as soon as it made an appearance in my mind. I didn't have time for a man in my life, in any way, shape, or form. Right now, my work was my life. It was up to me to continue Morley's legacy now. I didn't need any additional complications.

Getting married wasn't the best decision for me. It had been a favor a stranger, nothing serious.

Now it was over. It was time for me to leave and find Zelia's ladle.

My feet hit the ground, and I drew in a deep breath of warm night air. It tasted like freedom. I wasn't a prisoner in the house, but I didn't think he needed to be involved in my life. I wished I could stash the rope somewhere and hide my tracks, but in any event, it wouldn't take Ven long to figure out what happened. If he didn't know when I left or where I was going, he couldn't answer anyone's questions about my whereabouts.

Abel's men wouldn't hesitate to hurt Ven if they thought they could get to me through him. I wanted him completely out of the picture for his protection.

When I reached the edge of the property, I turned and shook my head at the big, empty house on the rock. It seemed lonely. Even though the exterior was beautiful, I could sense desolation beneath the surface.

Too bad things turned out this way.

There was a flight off the planet to Heralla tomorrow morning, and the next one wasn't until three days later. I had some things to do to get ready.

I didn't want to miss the spaceship. I didn't have any time to waste. I began slowly jogging toward the nearest major street.

Stars and possibility filled the night sky. I glanced up at them, smiling and feeling excited once I had left the dejected house that was not a home. I was moving toward the future and the accomplishment of a lifetime goal. I was finally getting somewhere and felt a sense of satisfaction for the first time since I had been forced to leave Heralla the first time.

I didn't look back.

CHAPTER 6

VEN

I tossed and turned, thinking about my life and wondering if I had ruined things by using TerraMates. Maybe I could have convinced one of my female friends to marry me and help me out. Surely it would have been easier than living with a stranger for the next year.

Something didn't sound right. I froze, holding perfectly still. There was noise coming from Emmy's room. I listened patiently for a moment, then got up and put my ear to her wall.

I wondered if she was ill, but the noise didn't sound biological. She was quiet. If I had been asleep, I wouldn't have heard a thing.

Click.

I frowned, wondering what could have made a sound like that in her room. It felt familiar, like something I had heard a hundred times before. Was it the closet door? Her suitcase, maybe? Something she brought with her?

My room was eerily quiet all of a sudden. If Emmy was awake, she must have gone back to sleep because I couldn't hear any more sounds coming from her room. I went back to my bed, full of curiosity about what she had been doing.

When I thought about it, I realized I knew nothing about my new wife. Perhaps she had other peculiar hobbies. I didn't know much about Earth women, but it seemed strange that she was interested in weapons. Despite our differences, apparently it was one thing we had in common. I had used guns frequently in the military, but I was familiar with physical weapons such as swords, daggers, and the bow and arrow.

Since I became independently wealthy, I had spent some time acquiring and learning how to use old Stalwartian weapons. I had even started fencing lessons. I had the time and the money, so I thought I should put it to good use. I set up a training dojo for practicing martial arts and working with a fencing instructor. A target for archery practice was located outside the dojo.

Sleep eluded me, so I decided I should use my time productively and run through my sword kata. I pulled off my pajama pants and donned a pair of shorts, leaving my chest bare. It was a warm night, and I would be hot soon enough. At the training studio, I picked up the meerkif hanging on the wall. It was a curved sword and a traditional weapon on Stalwart.

The meerkif was my favorite blade. It was heavy, but I was used to the balance. I hefted it and centered my weight correctly, assuming an opening stance. Taking a deep breath, I flipped the sword out, facing the blade away from me and carving an arc through the night air.

I lifted the weapon over my head and brought it down with a controlled swing. I slashed horizontally to the left and the right, moving backward each time.

When I finished the exercise, I bowed and replaced the sword on the wall. I padded slowly up the stairs in my bare feet, feeling calmer and more relaxed. Perhaps I would be able to sleep now.

As I lay in bed, about to drift off into a deep sleep, I realized what made the loud clicking noise. The epiphany jolted me awake.

The sound came from one of my largest climbing clips. I used it for hauling large amounts of cargo up and down cliffs. Stalwart was a rocky planet, and everyone knew how to climb. I knew it as well as I knew the sound of my voice, but I hadn't recognized it immediately due to the context.

Why would that sound be coming from Emmy's room?

I wasn't going get any sleep now. I hopped out of bed and was in the hall in seconds, positioning myself outside her door. My hand was poised to knock when I hesitated.

What if I imagined everything? Was she sleeping peacefully in bed at this moment? What if I woke her up, demanded to know about a vague clicking noise, and she told me to get the hell out of her room? It would not be an auspicious beginning to our union. Along with the chaste wedding night, it was shaping up to be an evening full of bad omens.

The security camera footage would let me see what was happening without disturbing her. It would also make me feel like a creep. It felt like invading her privacy and if she ever found out, she would be justifiably upset. Spying was out.

On the other hand, if something was wrong and she needed my help, I would kick myself for not going in sooner. My life had gotten pretty complicated in a few hours of marriage. I pressed my lips together and made a decision.

I knocked on the door and waited. I imagined Emmy would come sleepily to the door and ask me why I was bothering her. I had a story prepared that was mostly true. I could tell her I heard a suspicious noise in her room and wanted to investigate.

She would probably think I was coming in to seduce her. Would that be a bad thing?

The door wasn't opening. I waited, frowned at the door, and knocked again. No answer. When I tried opening the door, I discovered it was locked.

Either she was a sound sleeper or something was terribly wrong. What was happening inside that room? I scanned my retina on the lock, and the door slid silently open. I crept in quietly, not wanting to wake or disturb anyone in the room. It was dark and I felt like checking the window to make sure it was closed. The security system in the house was state-of-the-art, but you never knew what might happen.

I tripped and found myself falling onto my face, but I tucked and rolled at the last minute, avoiding a painful fall. I smiled to myself. The reflexes were still there.

Why had I tripped? I spoke a command to activate the lights, revealing a mess on the floor. I had tripped over one of my climbing ropes, which someone had clipped to the pole of the canopy bed. The line led to the window.

There wasn't a sign of Emmy anywhere.

Some of her clothes were still here, but her backpack was missing. I couldn't tell if she had taken any clothing with her, but it seemed clear she was gone. I didn't know where or why, but I had to get her back. Otherwise, this marriage would have been for nothing.

* * *

It took eight hours to retrieve the location of the gun. The information was available, but I had to go through a lot of government red tape to get it. If I had foresight, I wouldn't have needed to wait at all. I could have put a tracker under my control in the gun instead of relying on the government-provided chip. The decision could have saved me hours.

Instead, I had to wait until the office opened, then wait some more because there was a line of people in front of me. When it was finally my turn, I had been standing around for hours while someone else found my information and decrypted it. I never thought anyone would steal my weapon.

I stared at the screen, trying to interpret the data. The locator chip sent back information every ten minutes. I was looking at a map with flashing lights ranging from faint yellow all the way to dark red, showing where she had been. The brightest yellow indicated her first location and the red dot was a prediction of her current location.

After Emmy left my house, she made her way to the main city street. She made a couple of random stops, then headed directly to the spaceport. She intended to leave the planet.

The thought of her departure triggered a tremor in my heart. Why did that idea make my heart jump? I didn't know her. It didn't matter if she was my wife or not.

It seemed that she had moved around the spaceport. The darkest red dots showed her going away from the building again. Apparently she hopped into a car and was heading out onto the nearest freeway. That didn't make sense. If she was leaving the planet, why would she take a joyride back into the city? The next flight left in less than an hour.

I drew in a sharp breath and set the coordinates of my car to the loop outside the spaceport. Emmy was in trouble.

CHAPTER 7

EMMY

I adjusted the scarf, pulling it tighter around my head. I wished I was already on the spaceship. I purchased the scarf as a disguise. There wasn't a place at the spaceport to buy something which could dramatically alter my appearance. I had no idea whether Abel's men were still on the planet, but since they knew I was here, it made sense for them to keep watch on the spaceport. How else would I get off this world?

Unfortunately, the scarf itself was a little garish and conspicuous. It hid my hair and most of my face, at least. It would make me harder to spot from a distance.

I hadn't seen anyone yet, but I wasn't going to let my guard down. Abel had access to a lot of credits. He could easily pay for a couple of guys to watch the spaceport for a few days.

Morley and I had known Abel for a long time. There was a time when Abel followed the unwritten rules and played the game correctly. But as his wealth increased, he began to think rules didn't apply to him. Once he had enough money, Abel wasn't interested in credits any longer. He turned his attention to the acquisition of ancient objects.

Once he revealed that his goal was to amass a collection so vast that three blocks of warehouses couldn't hold it all. He was going to put everything on display for his eyes only. He claimed he had nothing else in his life.

Abel loved the hunt, tracking down clues and figuring out puzzles constructed to hide precious artifacts and keep them away from people like himself. The thrill of the hunt was what made his sorry life worthwhile to him.

I sighed and shifted from one foot to the other. I wondered if it was bad luck to think about Abel before I was safely away from his men. If I could get on this ship, I could catch the shuttle to Sector 72. I could easily get a ride to Heralla on a private spaceship from there, leaving no digital trace for Abel's men to follow.

As long as I could arrive with enough of a head start, I could retrieve the ladle and bring it to the authorities. I was steps away from freedom, only one person away from getting on the spaceship, when I felt two men flank me. One was blond. The other had a square jaw.

"Hey there," a blond man said in a soft voice. "Take off the scarf, pretty lady. Let us see your face."

I felt fear gnawing at my stomach. I was sure Abel's men surrounded me. "I have a scar. I'd rather keep my face private, if you don't mind."

"If we get her back to our room, she can take off more than just her scarf. The boss said she had to be alive. He wouldn't mind if we played with her a little."

"I get her first," the blond man said, whispering so he wouldn't attract attention.

"No way. I'm not getting seconds after you. Me first."

"We'll share her, then. She has three holes. Plenty of room for both of us."

The jackasses started laughing. I ignored them, thinking about how I could get out of here.

Making a scene might get them arrested, but it might not either. I had seen police officers turn and look the other way while Abel's men beat a guy and made him disappear. His money put him out of the law's reach. It was even possible they already paid off the spaceport security. Something had made them bold enough to come up to me in the middle of the line.

As an alternative, I could let them take me and have them think I had given up. Once they thought I was docile, I could pull out the weapon I took from Ven. I wondered if it was possible to steal from your husband. Didn't I own half of everything now?

They would take me somewhere, thinking they could use my body. I would stun them and run away. I put my hand into my pocket, reassuring myself the weapon was still there. I had previously set it to the highest level before a lethal shot. I didn't want to kill anyone if I didn't have to.

"I'll go with you." It didn't take much effort to sound terrified. "Please don't hurt me."

"Don't be scared, sweetie. It isn't going to hurt. You're going to be begging for more."

"It might hurt if we both take her together."

I tried not to vomit at the thought.

"Abel's got a private ship flying in here with more people, but it will take a while for it to arrive. There's plenty of time for some afternoon delight back at the hotel room. When the spaceship arrives, we'll get on the shuttle, and you'll show us the ladle of mystery. Once the boss man's got his stupid spoon, maybe he'll give me some time off."

I tried to convince myself that I had the upper hand. We wouldn't make it to the hotel.

"Let's go right now." The blond man was getting excited. I tried to keep calm and notice the details around me. It was often the smallest things that could make a big difference.

He bumped into me, his hand squeezing my breast as he turned me around. They kept me trapped between them all the way out of the spaceport, leading me into a waiting car. The blond guy leaned forward to set the destination while the other man started feeling me up. The car pulled away from the curb, and I struggled to remain calm. Would I even get a chance to go for the gun?

The guy with the square jaw pressed something onto my upper arm. I tried to wipe it off, but it dissolved into my skin before I could do anything. I didn't have time to figure out what he had done because I was beginning to realize I was in big trouble. Tomorrow's problems would have to take care of themselves.

"You know something? We don't have to wait until we get to the hotel. These windows are tinted." He called out a command to make the glass dark so no one could see in. "She can start with a blow job."

He began unbuckling his pants. I realized I had miscalculated. I thought I would have more time. The blond man sat back and without any warning, pulled my shirt over my head. I was left sitting between them wearing only a bra on top. At least it was a sports bra.

"Nice tits," the blond guy said. Square Jaw was struggling with his zipper, which seemed to be stuck.

"Hold her right there." After a minute, Square Jaw was finally able to unzip his pants. Getting dressed must have been a challenge for him in the morning.

I knew I had to act now, or it would be too late to change anything. I pulled out the gun and fired at Pants Impaired, who slumped back. The blond guy was so surprised that he didn't react right away. I'm not sure he even knew what happened.

I aimed the gun at the blond man, ready to test my luck again. Before I could fire, he knocked it out of my hand. I jumped toward the door and was about to open it when he moved in front of me and slammed it shut.

Shit.

He grabbed the gun and pointed it at me.

"Turn around slowly and I won't shoot you. It doesn't matter to me either way, though. A woman doesn't have to be conscious to get fucked." His tone was conversational.

What a bastard.

I turned, trying to figure out my next move as I rotated. I didn't want to get shot. Even if the gun was set to stun, it could still damage my nervous system. After being hit, people often found they couldn't walk or they lost control over their arms. I shuddered at the thought.

Another problem was that his gun might be set to lethal.

He was holding all the cards. I cursed myself for wasting my opportunity. I leaned against the door. I didn't want to give up, but I already felt defeated. If I couldn't even get off the planet, there was no way I was going to be able to get all the way to Heralla.

Unbidden, I heard Morley's voice in my head, just as I had heard it many times in life.

"You won't get anything by telling yourself you can't. Whatever you tell yourself, your mind will try to make a reality. Fill your head with things that will help you, not hinder you."

He always thought I was too negative. Maybe I was. Thinking about Morley made me put my chin up and look at the bastard in the eye. I was in a tight situation now, but I would get out of it.

"What now, sweetheart?" he said. "Are you going to come with me willingly or do I have to drag you away to have some fun?"

The lowest setting on the gun made people temporarily frozen. Much later, when they had regained the ability to move, their mind was groggy. A man must have designed the weapon. No one had realized they had created the perfect gun for rapists.

"Don't shoot me. I'll do whatever you want."

"That's quite a change of heart. I'm not sure I believe you. You killed my friend."

"He's not dead." I crossed my arms over my barely-covered breasts and rolled my eyes.

"When I checked him, he wasn't breathing." He looked scared but had a glimmer of hope in his eyes.

"A near-fatal stunning can cause a person to go into a practically catatonic state. The breathing rate slows down so much that you might not be able to see it. It doesn't mean he's dead."

"Is something the matter with you? You sound like a textbook!"

I shrugged. I had memorized some weapons specifications for a previous search. That was one thing that held my interest.

"You should check his pulse."

He slowly reached down to feel his companion's neck. I waited for an opportunity. When he dropped his eyes for a moment, trying to find the correct spot, I had my chance. His gun shifted and pointed in a different direction. Even if he fired his weapon the same instant I moved, it wouldn't hit me.

I lunged forward and smashed his hand, trying to either grab the gun or knock it away. He cursed, firing wildly. The blast missed me and hit the door. Something buzzed, and the aroma of burnt plastic filled the room. The idiot had fried the door shut.

We struggled against each other, both trying to get the gun. Then a thought occurred to me. What if he hadn't sealed the door shut but only damaged the computer controlling the lock? Even if the door wouldn't automatically open, the physical door handle might still work.

Of course, we were still speeding down a highway. Opening the door would lead to another set of problems.

The screen on my computer blinked, and I read a message, quickly twisting my forearm so my assailant couldn't see it. I stopped trying to grab the gun and felt around in a search for the door mechanism. When I found the handle, I pulled on it and the door opened. The wind rushed in, filling the vehicle with noise. It was a good thing my hair was tied back, or I wouldn't have been able to see anything. As it was, a few loose strands of my hair blew around wildly.

"What are you doing?" He didn't even try to grab me. "Are you crazy?"

"Maybe." I turned away and jumped out of the moving vehicle into traffic.

CHAPTER 8

EMMY

Before I jumped, I evaluated the distance between the two cars. Ven's message to me said to open the door. There weren't any additional instructions, but what else could I do except jump? As long as the car next to me kept an even speed, I thought I could make it.

I hoped there weren't any intersections ahead.

The distance between the two cars was small. The computers allowed them to drift much closer together than a biological driver could. I thought it was about two feet to the next car. Even though I didn't have far to jump, we were still speeding down the freeway. If I missed, I was as good as dead.

I didn't stop to think. I took a moment to envision myself landing safely and jumped, sailing through the air. I knew I was moving quickly, but during the time I was airborne everything seemed to slow down. When I tumbled through the open door of the other car, I crashed and fell into a heap.

Ven closed the door behind me immediately and told the car to move in a different direction. The vehicle shifted into another lane and exited the freeway. We were now driving on a road leading back to the spaceport.

It felt good to lie on the bottom of the car floor. I was still trying to make myself believe I was safe. My only regret was not getting to see the look on the blond guy's face. I missed it because I was focused on staying alive by jumping between two cars racing down a twenty-lane freeway.

"Emmy? Are you all right?" he asked, putting his hands on my shoulders and shaking me a little. His purple stripe seemed darker than before, and I wondered what made it change color.

I nodded, hoping I seemed calm.

All the fear of the past few days hit me at once, and I started to shake uncontrollably. I saw him search my face. It was easy to get lost in his eyes. Without warning, he pulled me into a tight embrace.

I surprised myself when I let him. I had never been held by a man before. My mom raised me. She was an only child, and her friends were all women. I had never had a real boyfriend, except Christopher. He was all about making out, not hugging.

I had no idea it could be such a pleasant experience.

My eyes closed and my arms moved by themselves, wrapping themselves around his waist. I buried my head into his chest and enjoyed the feeling of something bigger than myself.

His chest felt firm under my cheek. I loved how his arms held me closely like he was worried about me. Did he care for me? It seemed impossible because we had just met. I drew in a deep breath and let it out. The stress and tension left my body as his presence comforted me.

It felt good and safe. The sensation was so much like home that it scared me. The memory made my mind begin to function again, and I sat up, pulling away.

I smiled at him. Would he know that meant thank you? I sat back on the seats of the car. Ven turned to look at me directly. "Emmy, what are you doing?"

"Leaving?" I said hopefully.

"Why? We just got married. I wanted to get to know you." He glanced out of the window for a moment and looked at me again. "I thought you were going to stay."

"I married you because I thought I could do you a favor. It's nothing personal. I've helped you out, but I have a list of things to do myself for work. I'm sure you wouldn't be interested in it."

"Does your work usually involved being kidnapped?"

Shit. "My job can be dangerous sometimes."

"What's the job? You should be able to explain that, at least. Are you ex-military?" Ven had an odd expression on his face.

"No way." I laughed at his misunderstanding. "Not that kind of dangerous."

"If you could give me a kernel of truth, it would explain a lot."

"I've been honest. I told you everything I said would be the truth. There were some things I don't feel comfortable talking about."

"You said you'd see me in the morning." He looked unhappy. "That seems deceptive, at the least."

"Not really. I'm seeing you right now," I pointed out.

"Why did you climb out the window instead of using the door?"

"I didn't want you to know when I left. I thought using the window would make it harder for you to find me."

"That seems reasonable, but you should have read up about Stalwart's weapon licensing regulations. If you didn't want anyone to locate you, it was a mistake to take a gun with a built-in tracking chip. I wish I could have been here sooner."

"I would have figured something out. I always find a way. No worries."

"No worries?" He said the words in an intimidating tone. His purple stripe nearly became black. I shifted away from him, not wanting to take the brunt of an outburst. "I think they were going to kill you, Emmy. They were trying to kidnap you, weren't they?"

He looked at me for confirmation. I thought about their threats and shuddered. "You're half-right. They were going to take me somewhere against my will." I wrinkled my nose in disgust. "But they won't kill me."

"How do you know that?"

"They have to keep me alive. I have some information they need."

He shook his head. "It better be information that can save the galaxy, that's all I have to say."

"It's complicated, and it's not your problem. If you could let me take care of a few issues, I could return and pose as your wife for a while, if it would help you out."

"That's not how it works. We have to live together and be together. If you go off somewhere for some undetermined time, the executors will assume I only married you to keep my uncle's fortune."

"They're remarkably perceptive," I murmured.

He made a face at me. "They'll declare the marriage a sham, and the entire exercise will have been pointless." His voice sounded like he was losing hope. Part of me felt bad that I was deserting him in a time of need. But I had no reason to help him any longer.

"I'm sorry, Ven. I wish I could help you more. Would it help if you faked my death?"

When the words left my mouth, blasts of laser fire hit the side of the car, making it start to swerve wildly on the empty back road. Abel's men were back, and they meant business. Maybe Ven wouldn't have to fake my death after all.

* * *

VEN

Emmy was nuts. Why would she want me to fake her death? I had a good plan, and she had blown it to pieces with a single crazy jump.

My idea was simple. I wanted to get my car close to hers, shoot any unwanted passengers, and pull her body across to safety. As soon as her door opened, she judged the distance and jumped between the cars. I did a lot of military operations where I had to move my body through the air, but even I would think twice before leaping to my doom. Emmy didn't even think once.

I was about to say I couldn't fake her death when the car shook. A giant cannon was attacking us. I pulled Emmy down to the floor as the glass started to shatter.

These guys were bastards. Emmy said they wouldn't kill her, but I thought she was wrong. Our car swerved wildly all over the empty road. We were fortunate to be off the main highway. At best, they wouldn't intentionally murder her, but considering their giant weapons they could easily have an accident.

More importantly, they wouldn't care at all if they killed me. I hadn't survived ten years in the Stalwart military to die at the hands of random Earth goons.

"Tell the car to go back to the spaceport. Let's head for one of the staff entrances."

I opened the window and leaned out, holding the gun. With deliberate care, I aimed and hit a spot I knew would destroy their battery. All the cars on Stalwart ran on solar energy, which was renewable and good for the planet, but left them vulnerable to attacks on their power systems. Their vehicle began to fall back immediately. It would take them a few minutes to get the auxiliary battery online. By that time, I hoped we would be back in the spaceport.

They half-heartedly shot a few more times at our vehicle, forcing me to duck inside. Soon their car was out of range, and their guns were useless. We turned off into a back alley leading to a small door marked for employees only. We clambered out of the car. I keyed in another destination. It sped off by itself as soon as we shut the doors.

I ran up to the door and pulled out a device to open it. It would give me temporary clearance and wouldn't leave a digital trail. I brought a few of my fancier gadgets with me when I realized I was going on a rescue mission. The door opened, and Emmy followed me without saying a word. I think she finally understood the gravity of her situation.

Once inside, we rushed past people getting ready for work or coming off their shift. I tried to look friendly and like I belonged here, smiling at people and saying hi. When we exited the employee room, we found ourselves in the heart of the spaceport. It was a deserted region where no ships were scheduled to leave. Across the open room was a maintenance door. I grabbed Emmy's hand, pulling her across the area.

Something happened when I touched her hand. A pulse of energy raced up my arm. It was like nothing I had ever experienced before. I glanced back, wondering if she had felt anything unusual. Her eyes looked surprised, and she stared at her fingers. My hand tingled in the middle of my palm. I didn't think about letting go until a group of five men and a dangerous-looking woman burst out of the employee door.

We ducked through a maintenance hatch. "How did they follow us here?" Emmy asked.

"They probably put a tracker on you. It's the simplest explanation. There's no other way they could have known which direction we went."

"There's nothing on me, is there?" She stopped to look at herself.

I followed her gaze and felt a shot of lust go directly to my cock. She was wearing the same tight, curve-hugging black pants as yesterday, but her shirt had vanished. Somehow I had missed this vital fact because I was so worried about keeping her out of danger.

She only wore a sports bra. Her generous breasts showed a fair amount of cleavage. Now that I was taking the time to inspect her body, I realized Emmy didn't carry extra weight. Her body had large breasts and swelling hips. But her waist was narrow. Looking at that bare skin made me want to put my hands on her hips and pull her close to me.

I forced my gaze away from her body. I didn't want to get distracted by her physical appearance. I reminded myself that she was annoyingly intelligent and possibly genuinely crazy. I had never seen anyone jump from car to car before. Emmy was the most maddening woman I could remember meeting, and she was not the type of woman with whom I ever wanted to get involved.

My moment of fantasy was interrupted when her pursuers spotted us. We had to run. I pulled Emmy through the maintenance door, and we immediately crashed into someone coming through from the other side.

"What are you doing?" he yelled. He grabbed Emmy and pulled out a gun. Belatedly, I noticed he wore a spaceport security uniform.

Fuck.

I put my hands in the air as he waved the gun in my direction.

"We don't want any trouble." We were already in trouble. In about a minute, the people chasing Emmy were going to come through that door. We were sitting ducks.

CHAPTER 9

VEN

I wasn't sure what the right thing to do was. I wasn't prepared to risk being stunned. I wouldn't be any good to Emmy if I were unconscious. Spaceport security was known for being trigger-happy.

As it turned out, I didn't need to do anything. Emmy rotated, throwing her body weight behind her fist and punching a hard uppercut to the chin. She hit him so strongly that she pushed his head back.

He swore. Emmy had already twisted her other hand out of his grip. She drove a right hook into his temple that knocked him out cold.

I stared in surprise. I knew women who could fight. I served with plenty of women who were tougher than me. However, it was disconcerting to see my wife beating up an out-of-shape, middle-aged security guard.

Emmy caught me looking at her. "Do you have a problem? I know how to take care of myself."

She certainly did. Her words were enough to break me out of my trance. "Let's go." I pulled her behind me.

"Earlier in the car they put something on my upper arm. I think it was the tracker. Do you know how to get rid of it?"

"Something?" I asked as we ran, dodging workers and equipment. I heard someone behind us come through the door and crash into the security guard Emmy had just punched. He was having a bad day.

"Was it a cream?" If someone spread a tracer cream on her body, they would be able to track her location for days. I had a device that would scramble the tracer's signal, but I couldn't activate it right now.

We dashed to the right, moving down an empty hallway. I was impressed that she could run this far without running out of breath. She must be in good shape. And her abs were beginning to turn me on. I had never been into women who worked out excessively. I thought I liked my women naturally thin and on the soft side. Emmy was starting to grow on me with her fit, healthy body. If I weren't running for my life, my cock would be hard.

What was I thinking? I needed to focus before the bastards behind us took Emmy away. That would wreak havoc with my plan and her life. Because as soon as they got any information from her, she would no longer have any value to them and they would kill her. That wasn't going to happen. I had sworn to protect her. Whether she wanted me to or not, I was going to do my duty.

"Let's go in there." She pointed to a door that read *Docking Bay #12*. The line of doors down the hallway stretched away from us, with numbers that seemed to advance all the way to infinity, but I knew there were only about ninety docking bays. We were at the main spaceport for Stalwart. Almost all of the shuttles coming to the planet passed through this building.

I opened the door and ran through, turning and locking it behind us. Thirty seconds later, we heard it rattle and bang from the other side. We didn't stop as we ducked around the spacecraft.

We heard the sound of blaster fire, and the door exploded. Five people barged into the docking bay, which seemed deserted except for us and our pursuers.

"Where did they go?"

I didn't hear anyone answer. Emmy and I continued to move around the shuttlecraft looking for anything that could help us. We needed to find a place to hide or a way to get out of the docking bay. As we crept through the shuttles, I started a program on my computer that would block the signal coming from the tracer on Emmy's body.

We couldn't find another way out. We were either leaving through the same door we entered or out the giant door for spaceships. Neither option sounded good. A man was guarding the other side of the door, and I didn't want to roast inside the engines of a ship.

"How long will the tracker remain active?"

"The blocker takes a few minutes to start working. If they used a cream on you, the effects are temporary."

"That's not reassuring. They can still track me right now?"

"Yes. It will be harder for them to find you. But it's the only way they could know we were in this particular bay."

We needed to find a better hiding place quickly.

Emmy eagerly tried all the door handles we passed to see if any hapless souls had left them unlocked. We got lucky. A door led into a mid-sized private spaceship. She beckoned to me, and we both slipped inside, pulling the door shut. A moment later we heard footsteps approaching our location.

Even though we were trying to be quiet, we had not closed the door tightly. We wanted to listen to any movements of people trying to find us. Emmy and I positioned ourselves on either side of the door. Neither one of us dared to take a step or make any noise.

The narrow entrance to the spacecraft was tight. If I moved another inch closer to her, her breasts would brush against my chest.

I tried to ignore her proximity. I focused on controlling my breathing until it was calm and quiet again. The footsteps came closer. I heard someone pull on door handles.

They would reach our spaceship in a minute. When they did, it would be obvious our door was open. I prepared to fight, flexing and releasing my muscles.

I waited for the door to fly open when a loud voice came from the vicinity of the docking bay door.

"What are you doing in here?" There was a pause until the voice start yelling. "Security! I need security here right now!"

We heard the sounds of a scuffle followed by silence.

I let out my breath. Emmy and I looked at each other. She motioned her head toward the interior of the ship. I nodded, hoping I could understand her without any explanation. The spaceport worker had bought us some time, but we weren't out of trouble yet.

* * *

EMMY

I noticed Ven was good-looking before I married him. But once I found out that he was an annoying, stuck in his life, stuffy billionaire, I lost interest. It didn't matter how sexy he was.

I didn't have anything against wealthy aliens, but he wasn't the guy for me. I didn't need a man at all. But if I were going to pick someone for myself, it wouldn't be an alien who pursued his interests all day and would do anything to maintain the status quo.

83

Anyone who wanted to be with me needed an interest in adventure. I was an archeologist who hunted down precious treasures, and there wasn't anything normal about my life. I loved it, but I knew it wasn't for everyone. I couldn't imagine being with someone like Ven. He was so desperate to keep his life the way it was that he would marry a stranger.

Right now, I wondered if there was more to Ven than I had originally thought. He certainly handled the gun smoothly. The shot from a moving car to take out the other car's batteries had been difficult. It took a lot of practice to be that accurate with a civilian weapon.

Today he wore casual clothes. I don't know if Earth was exporting its clothing styles to Stalwart, but he wore a tight T-shirt on top that showed off an incredible body with well-defined biceps and a broad chest. His bare arms had a purple stripe here and there in different locations, and I momentarily wondered if there were any markings on his cock.

My mind wouldn't stop. I remembered when he took my hand. Fireworks ignited inside of me that went straight to my core. I might not have noticed all of Ven's attributes yesterday, but I was certainly seeing them today.

I took a chance and stole a quick peek at him for a moment as we moved through the spaceship's dim interior. He stared back at men without speaking. He was talking volumes with dark eyes that seemed to hold many secrets.

I didn't mind secrets. I had some of my own. There was something about Ven that made me want to discover the answer to every one of his. I wanted to know what made him tick. I wanted to understand him. And I guess I wanted to fuck him, too.

My knees had felt weak when we waited at the door together, hoping no one would find us. There were so many different emotions pulsing through my body that I could hardly sort them out. Fear had been predominant, but there was longing too and a desire to be closer to him. If I had only moved one more inch, we would have touched chest-to-chest.

"How about in here?" he whispered, opening the door to a cargo space. There were several large cartons providing cover. "I don't think they'll search every ship. The person they knocked out already alerted security. The cops should be here soon. Even if they do explore this ship before security arrives, we'll have a chance to shoot whoever comes through the door."

I nodded. "Okay."

We shut the door behind us. There was a round window at one end of the room and two jump seats that could be pulled down for additional passengers. The extra seats had restraints. I imagined this area was where the workers stayed during take-off. This spaceship had a lot of bells and whistles. It was a luxurious personal vessel, and I imagined a rich and famous Stalwartian owned it.

"When things settle down out there, we can sneak out and make our escape. I'm going to increase the power of the signal scrambling their tracer. It should make it harder for them to track you."

"Sounds like a plan." I sat on the floor and tried to slow down my racing pulse. Ven hovered next to me. I was acutely aware of his presence. He was just close enough to touch me, but he was careful to leave a little distance, like an invisible barrier. Ven typed some information into his computer until he felt satisfied and sat back.

Adrenaline filled me after our race through the spaceport. Having Ven so close to me was doing interesting things to my libido.

I had never even been interested in a *human* male before. I was attracted to certain actors, and there was one person in school who I daydreamed about, but those were all fantasies. It was entirely different when I wanted a male who was right beside me and who might be thinking about me too. That had never happened to me before. I wondered if I had always secretly yearned for an alien to sweep me off my feet.

Nah. I was probably just too busy.

Merely making it to university had been a challenge. I finished high school when I was seventeen and worked two jobs, studying the rest of the time to pass my classes. After university, it was more school all the time.

I never had time for a man. I could have had a boyfriend when I was working on my Ph.D., but no one was interested in me at the time. If they were, I wasn't interested in them.

All of a sudden, I felt insecure. I had never been in this situation before, and I didn't know what to do. Should I kiss him?

"Emmy." Ven stared straight ahead.

The sound of his voice brought me out of my daydream and back to reality.

"What?" I felt nervous. How old was he, anyway? He looked like he was a few years older than me, but the way he was acting right now made him seem even older than I had thought. He turned his head and he had an intimidating look in his black eyes.

"You are going to tell me everything immediately." I couldn't look away. I knew he was right. I tried as hard as I could to keep him out of my mess of a life, but he was here despite my best efforts. Now his life was in danger. He had a right to know.

"This is going to sound strange, but there's a ladle. It's all the ladle's fault."

CHAPTER 10

VEN

I closed my eyes, shutting out the view of the cargo hold. With my vision cut off, I could smell a faint stuffy odor. The shuttle had taken a long space flight recently, and they hadn't had the time to recycle the air. When I drew a deep breath in through my nose, I caught a whiff of Emmy's scent. The fragrance was both sweet and foreign in an intriguing way.

"A ladle? You mean, like a spoon for dishing out soup?" I stared at her blankly, knowing my face was a mask of disbelief.

She sighed, looking down at her knees which were drawn up to her chest. The position of her legs crushed her breasts and made them temptingly bulge up out of her bra.

One of the drawbacks of tall, skinny women is that they have small breasts. All of my former women had been deficient in their chest. I couldn't stop staring at her breasts, which rose and fell as she breathed. My mind wondered what it would feel like to hold her plump mounds in my hands and take one red bud into my mouth. What color were her nipples?

Did I want her nipples in my mouth? Wasn't this woman crazy? If I was honest with myself, I had to admit that I wanted her breasts and much more. But I couldn't let myself get carried away with Emmy. I was sure she was more trouble than she was worth. I just needed her to stay with me for a year as I had planned with Montana.

After we had finished our time together, it wouldn't matter if she needed to go somewhere for work or personal business. We had to live in the same residence. It was a big house, and we wouldn't get in each other's way.

I reluctantly drew my attention away from her breasts. How could all this nonsense be because of a magical spoon?

She gave me a rueful smile. "If it weren't for the Silver Mestolo of Zelia, or informally, Zelia's ladle, I wouldn't be here right now. I would probably be working in a museum on Earth, cleaning dirt off arrowheads."

"Emmy." I tried to restrain my temper. The woman was irritating but simultaneously so attractive that I didn't know what to think. "Try to say something that makes sense soon, or..." I broke off, not sure what I would do, but imagined it would involve our bodies pressing together.

"Or what?" She glared at me with a challenge in her eye.

I knew Montana would never have looked at me like that. She would have agreed with me. I always selected a particular type. Genial, agreeable, wanting to please...that sort of woman. Not the kind to openly challenge me and push my buttons.

I decided to start over. "Please allow me to rephrase myself. I don't know how long we have. I'm not that smart, and I would like a clear explanation."

"The Silver Mestolo. It's a word in an ancient Earth language that means ladle. The first woman who discovered its existence was a famous archeologist from Earth named Zelia. It's made from filaden, one of the strongest elements in the galaxy. Even if you dropped a spaceship on it, the Mestolo wouldn't be crushed." She trailed off when she saw the look on my face.

"It's a serving instrument. I get it. But why does everyone want it?"

"Morley believes it can cure any disease. It contains a large concentration of Higgs boson particles. On Earth, we think Higgs boson particles are the source of matter and life."

It took everything within me not to smile. This human was talking about Higgs boson particles like they were the first ones to discover them. The commonly accepted name for them was Trovveqs.

Emmy mentioning Trovveqs meant she was highly educated...for an Earth woman. I wondered how intelligent she was. She was much different than I had imagined Montana. I had anticipated conversations about riding and making small talk with my wife, not speaking about physics.

"The Zelia's ladle has a higher concentration of these particles, and the theory is that it can enhance the life of anyone who drinks from it," she finished. "It may be able to heal patients previously thought to be incurable."

My mind was only partially listening to her words. The other half contemplated Emmy's education. Even though she came from a primitive planet like Earth, apparently she was one of its most highly educated inhabitants.

I had old feelings of inadequacy from when my aunt repeatedly told me I was stupid. I couldn't help it. Whenever I found myself around people smarter than me, I felt like an idiot. I tried to focus on what Emmy was saying, but I had a terrible feeling in my gut.

At the same time, I fixated on her soft, pink lips. Perhaps if I kissed her, she'd stop talking about Higgs boson particles and bringing up my old issues. But I couldn't kiss her because I wasn't going to get involved with her.

What kind of guy couldn't handle having a woman who was smarter than him? A pathetic one.

* * *

EMMY

I tried to ignore how close Ven was to my body. I knew I owed him an explanation. I couldn't sum up everything in three sentences. He was getting annoyed with my vague statements. I had to start at the beginning, or the motivations of the people involved would be confusing.

His arm was touching me, and I could feel warmth and tingles at the point of contact. When I was this close to him, I couldn't deny the attraction. In fact, I could hardly focus on my story. Energy rose in my torso and spread out, making me feel giddy. I forced myself to concentrate on how I had ended up here.

"Everything started when I was still a little girl. My mentor and teacher, Morley, began searching for Zelia's ladle. He had been searching for it for about twenty-two years when I met him. I was a graduate student in archeology at the top of my class."

Ven wrinkled his nose. I realized I probably didn't need to add the part about being the best.

"He hired me to work with him when I finished school. I started as an assistant and worked my way up."

"Because you both became obsessed with a utensil?"

I scowled. "We weren't obsessed," I said, objecting to a word that implied I was nuts. "We were enthusiastic."

He stared at me.

"Persistent?"

No response.

"Okay, driven. But not obsessed."

"You sound like treasure hunters to me."

I pressed my lips together. That was the most insulting thing he could have said to me. I didn't like to be called a treasure hunter. It made me feel gauche. Treasure hunters were classless money-grubbing jerks. I thought of myself as a sophisticated archeologist. With a single comment, Ven had implied that Morley's work was an obsession, and my assistance said the same thing about me.

I resolved to control my temper.

"Morley pieced together many clues about the ladle. He worked on it between paying projects until he had enough information to start an expedition. We were close. We narrowed it down to a single planet and thought a mountain concealed it. I got sick and had to go back to Earth. Morley continued without me."

I glanced up at him quickly. Did he think I was a coward? I wondered if he had anything to say but he only lifted his chin, indicating for me to continue.

"Once I had recovered enough to speak again, we talked every day. We discussed his progress and tried to decipher the riddle of Zelia's ladle. One day was different."

I didn't think about Morley's death often, but whenever I did, I choked up. I tried to pull myself together. I knew Morley wouldn't want me crying over him. I couldn't help it. I missed him so much.

"He was a father figure to me. I never knew my dad." I didn't know why I needed to explain my emotions, but I couldn't stop talking. Ven patiently waited as I wiped my eyes.

"He called me one day with a cryptic message and then the men who were chasing him..." The tears were falling again. "They caused a cave-in somehow and killed him. I never heard from Morley again. Morley died, and all his knowledge vanished."

I sat silently, absorbed in my memories and thinking about my loss. I wasn't the only one affected. Morley's death hurt the archeological community as well.

"Everything wasn't lost. You're still here. Part of Morley lives through you."

I stared at the floor. "That's right." I lifted my eyes again. "The last transmission he sent me held a key to finding the ladle. It has something to do with the Stone Goddess of Heralla."

"And you want to get it?" His tone sounded condescending.

"I don't want to. I'm going to. Morley entrusted me with information that could find the artifact and save descendants of the Great Race all across the galaxy. Nothing's going to stand in my way."

"Do you think an old ladle is going to save people?" He looked at me like I was nuts. "Let me guess. It makes a magic soup."

I tried to explain patiently, remembering that everyone didn't have the same knowledge I did.

"Sort of. There is supposed to be an abnormally high concentration of Higgs-Boson particles in the ladle's metal. Legends say it can cure almost any ailment."

"Really." He looked skeptical.

"Yes. That's why Morley was interested in it. He wanted the ladle for his brother who had an incurable disease. Medical science has made fantastic advances, but there are still neurological diseases that our doctors can't cure. Even if Zelia's ladle can't fix everything, it should provide medical researchers with fresh ideas."

"If what you're saying is true, it would be amazing."

"I know. Morley knew this brother would eventually become a vegetable if he didn't find it. His brother was the most important person in the world to him, even after they had a falling out."

"That must have been difficult."

"I don't know much about it, to tell you the truth. Morley rarely spoke about his brother. I knew he was hurt, but even after whatever happened, Morley still wanted to find the ladle."

"So who were the guys chasing after him? Am I right in assuming they're the same men who were trying to take you?"

I nodded. "Those were Abel's men. He's another person looking for Zelia's ladle. He'll do almost anything to get it."

"Who's Abel?" Ven looked confused again.

"Abel wants to keep the silver Zelia's ladle and keep it for himself. He's the one who sent the men to me. There's one more thing." I hesitated, bitterness filling my heart as I remembered.

"He killed Morley."

CHAPTER 11

EMMY

The sound of voices outside the space shuttle made my stomach flip. I held my breath until they moved away.

Ven shook his head. I wondered if he was troubled by my story, or if he didn't believe anything I was saying.

"He killed Morley?"

"At the minimum, he indirectly caused Morley's death." I was beginning to feeling defensive. "It was as good as killing him. He was the one who gave the order to use explosives and empty the tunnel. It destabilized the area, resulting in a cave-in around the section Morley was searching."

I closed my eyes, feeling silent tears beginning to drip down my cheeks. It still hurt. I missed him. My heart ached for the man who had been more of a father to me than my genetic parent, who had abandoned me.

I shouldn't have been surprised, but I jumped when I felt Ven put his arms around me and pull me close to him. I let out a shuddering sigh.

Why did everything seem less horrible when he had his arms around me? It didn't make sense.

I wrapped my arms around him, his comforting presence giving me permission to unleash all the feelings I had held back ever since Morley died. I sobbed until my heartache went away.

When I recovered, I was soaking an alien I hardly knew with my tears. "I'm sorry."

"Don't be." He held on and wasn't letting go.

"I'm not in the habit of crying on the shoulders of strangers, Ven."

I broke off what I was saying when he put his hand under my chin and forced my face up. What I saw on his face made me freeze with my whole body at attention.

"You don't have to be sorry." He was searching my eyes for something. I don't know what he found, but a heartbeat later, he leaned down, and I experienced my first real kiss.

A quick peck in the bathroom at a childhood birthday party didn't count. Kissing Christopher had been like giving mouth-to-mouth to a snake. I had only done it because I thought he wanted me to, not because I enjoyed it.

This was different.

The feeling of his lips touching mine took my breath away while simultaneously setting off fireworks in my body. I forgot that I didn't want a man. I forgot that I had to focus on my goal. I think I even forgot my name.

I held him tighter, making a little sound in the back of my throat and opening my mouth so that our tongues could touch.

How could something that sounded so weird be this amazing?

His arms were roaming over my back and found the hem of my shirt. I felt his hot palms slipping underneath my clothes and lightly grazing the skin of my torso. I practically passed out from the pleasure of his touch. I didn't think the kiss could get any hotter and yet somehow it did.

But when his hands moved up and one brushed the side of my breasts, making me shudder, I realized what I was doing.

"Ven." I pulled away as I gasped his name.

"What?" He closed his eyes, as if in pain. He put his hand to his forehead and started to rub it. I noticed that he had two thin purple stripes on the back of his right hand, almost like a cat had clawed him. "I know. I shouldn't have done that."

"No, you shouldn't have. Isn't there a no-sex clause?"

He opened his eyes and looked at me in amusement. "We weren't having sex. At least, that's not what they call it on my planet."

"No, but kissing leads to sex. Everyone knows what happens when you start kissing, pretty soon you're naked and things start happening."

"I do know." The look in his eyes made me melt again. That made one of us. I blushed.

"I'm not going to lie, Emmy. I'd like to see you naked."

I felt my eyes widen, and there was a gush of wetness between my legs. Was that normal? I knew nothing about sex. I would have to read up on the subject.

I wasn't going to have sex with Ven, was I?

"That would definitely lead to sex. We're not having sex because our marriage is barely legal."

"No?" he asked, his eyes smoldering. He flipped over my forearm and ran his finger along my skin, revealing the embedded marriage certificate. His touch made me shiver. "This looks pretty real to me."

"You know what I mean, Ven."

"If you don't want to have sex with me, you don't have to. That's one of the stipulations in the contract."

"I know that. It's not that I don't want to…"

"So you do want to have sex with me. What's the problem?"

I pressed my lips together and huffed out my breath, staring at the ceiling in embarrassment. I had to admit to myself that my body seemed ready to participate. But my mind told me that I was smarter than that.

Besides, he wouldn't want someone inexperienced like me.

He studied me for a long moment and he must have read my mind. He spoke his next words in an incredulous tone of voice.

"Wait a second, Emmy. Are you still a maiden?"

"A maiden?" I frowned, then understanding dawned on my face. "Oh, you mean a virgin?" My cheeks were burning up.

"How old are you?" He flipped my arm over again to check my birth date on the marriage certificate. I pulled away, but not before he starts doing the calculation in his head. "Wow!"

"Shut up," I said. "I never planned on getting married. I don't want a man."

"Oh, so you like girls?" Now it was his turn to blush.

"A lesbian? No." I was frustrated that I couldn't articulate what I meant. He had me flustered after the kiss.

"That's a relief."

"Would there be something wrong if I were?" I asked, taking offense on behalf of lesbians everywhere.

"Of course not. The kiss felt like you were extremely interested, that's all. I would be an idiot if I couldn't tell a woman's interest in me."

"I'm interested," I muttered. "I just don't want to be."

"You're attracted to me, but you don't want to be? What the hell does that mean? I thought Earth women would be less confusing than the women on my planet."

"I think women are the same everywhere. It's nothing personal, but I don't need a man to be happy. I don't want the complications that come with a relationship, okay? I like you well enough. It's not that. And you're…"

"What?"

I shrugged. "Hot. But I don't think it's a good idea for us to get involved sexually."

"I agree." He still looked put out.

"You do?" I was taken aback by his sudden acceptance.

"You're right. I shouldn't have done that. I apologize. If you want me in your bed, Emmy, you'll have to make the first move. From now on, we're totally platonic."

He looked like he was annoyed with the whole situation, or maybe only with himself for getting carried away. I had no idea why he was irritated, but something was bothering him.

"You're not my type, anyway," he added, almost to himself.

It felt like a slap in the face, but I remembered the appearance of the woman with whom I traded tickets in the spaceport. She had been tall, thin, and blonde…nothing like me. If she was his type, then I probably wasn't.

"You're not my type either. I suppose we're done with this nonsense then."

He nodded curtly and stood up. The sound of his boots on the metal floor of the ship hollowly echoed as he moved away from me. I didn't know where he was going, and I didn't care. I just wanted to be somewhere else.

I rose and walked in the opposite direction, going to look at the window. My feelings were stupid. I didn't know this guy. It was impossible that he could have hurt my feelings by rejecting me, especially when I didn't want to have sex with him either.

He hadn't said anything about fucking. Apparently he wanted to see me naked. But I wasn't his type, and he wasn't my type. It was going to be a purely platonic relationship, which was fine by me. I didn't need the complications Ven would bring to my life.

But if that was all true, then why did I feel disappointed?

* * *

VEN

My head felt like it might explode. My cock, too. This woman was driving me crazy. All I wanted was to learn why those guys were chasing her. Instead, I got a tutorial on the history of the Silver Mestolo of Zelia and the story of Emmy's whole life.

I don't know what made me put my arms around her. It was a mistake. And yet, when I thought about it again, it hadn't felt like a mistake. It felt good. Like I had been missing something all my life.

Is that feeling why Pan always went home to Jalla instead of staying for one more beer at the bar? I had always thought he was whipped. Now I suspected it was something else, an elusive feeling that you couldn't find hanging out with your friends.

It was a sense of rightness that penetrated to my bones. The idea that as long as she was with me, nothing was as bad as I imagined. I thought I could hold her and take away her pain. Is this what made happily married guys abandon the fun of one-night stands and the free life of a bachelor?

I had only met Emmy recently. We didn't even know each other. Why had I let her cry on my shoulder? More importantly, why hadn't it felt awkward? If any other woman had cried on me, I would have run as far as I could to get away, no matter who was waiting outside.

At the time, I didn't want to run. I had wanted to kiss her tears away and make love to her until she forgot her aching heart and cried out my name.

"Holy fuck," I said out loud, surprised by my thoughts. Had this woman put a spell on me? I was not interested in falling in love. Ever since the love of my life left me five years ago, I had managed to keep all the women I slept with at arm's length, never dating them long enough to form a connection.

How had Emmy snuck into my heart already?

I pressed my hands against the wall of the ship and touched my forehead to the cool metal, trying to make sense of all the emotions that were churning inside of me.

I would keep her away just like all the other women. Montana would have stayed at arm's length, where I wanted her. When I decided to contact TerraMates, I imagined an agreeable companion. A bed buddy. Some nice eye candy across the table from me every morning. I had wanted an easy, no-strings-attached and straightforward relationship.

When I thought about Emmy's dark eyes gazing at me, and the feeling of her lips against me, I realized it might be too late to stay arm's length apart. The only thing my arms wanted to do was go back and wrap her in them again. I formed fists with my hands, trying to remove the desire to hold her.

Now what was I going to do?

CHAPTER 12

EMMY

I needed to talk to Ven. I had made a mistake.

My body and mind immediately revolted against the idea that the most incredible moment of my life had been a mistake. I tried to ignore them.

We had made a mistake...that I wanted to make with him again and again.

I tried to gain control over my unruly libido. Things didn't have to be awkward. We were both adults and could still be friends in spite of the memory of a scorching hot, passionate kiss burning between us.

I didn't want to think about the kiss, but the memory kept sneaking up on me when I least expected it. I remembered the heat of his mouth and energy shooting through my body. I remembered how hard his chest was and the way he possessed me. I was out of control like never before, and it felt good and right.

Maybe it was just bad timing.

We certainly had different life plans. It didn't make sense to get involved with anyone right now. I had always lived my life in a methodical, logical way. Ven didn't fit into the structure.

Right now, I had to talk to him and arrange to get off this damn planet. Preferably without Abel's men knowing about it. I tiptoed to where he lurked around a corner of the L-shaped room.

"Ven, we need to talk."

"Shhh." He put his finger to his lips. "Someone's coming."

I looked out of the window and gasped. Abel's men were outside, and they were approaching the ship.

"I thought you scrambled the tracer signal?" I asked. He shrugged.

"Either their devices are incredibly sensitive, or the scrambler failed. I'm not an electronics genius."

I heard the sound of voices moving to the outside door. A door opened, and someone entered the ship.

"Do we have any options?" I asked, not particularly eager to hear the answer.

"We can hide. If they find us, we shoot them. If they don't find us and they leave, then we can get out of here."

"And get me a ticket off this planet," I added.

He sighed but didn't say anything as he walked over to a large closet.

"We can discuss it once we're out of this situation." He opened the door to the closet, which looked small and uninviting when I imagined stuffing my body inside. "Get in."

∗ ∗ ∗

VEN

I should have thought of a better place to conceal ourselves. Instead of being able to sneak off the shuttlecraft and take Emmy home to discuss her future, we were stuck hiding together in a closet.

Whenever I inhaled, my lungs filled with her scent. The fragrance seemed delicious and unrecognizable. It was probably an aroma from Earth. Underneath the initial odor, I detected the smell of her arousal. I didn't need another distraction. I stopped breathing as much as possible and tried to focus on something else, but Emmy was the only thing around.

We had squeezed into the closet and faced each other with only six inches of air separating us. It was way too close, especially considering that we had recently decided to stop touching each other.

It didn't matter what I said. Imagining her body next to me and her intoxicating scent was making my cock ache. The only thing I wanted to do was strip her and fuck her, right here.

I needed to keep my mind thinking about anything except what I wanted to do to her. For a few more minutes, at least. Once I had some distance, I would feel differently. Being stuck in close quarters with her was maddening.

Emmy took a deep breath. I watched her cleavage rise and fall in the dim light. I stared at her breasts, entranced by the sight. I wondered what she would look like when I made her come. And whether she would make a noise in her throat again if I kissed her.

We could talk, I supposed. That would take my mind off Emmy and what I wanted to do with her.

I hoped.

"Em, let me make sure I've got this straight." She looked up at me, her eyes a little unfocused as if she were returning from somewhere far away. I hadn't meant to use the diminutive form of her name. It slipped out but somehow it felt right. "You are bound and determined to get a ladle for your friend and colleague, Morley."

"Zelia's ladle. I promised him before he died."

"After you get this artifact, you're not going to make soup with it. You're going to give it to the authorities so they can use it for everyone's benefit, but Abel's men will be chasing you every step of the way."

Her eyes shifted away from mine.

"Not every step. I've been able to take care of myself until now. If I can get a head start, I'll be fine."

"Won't they guess you're going to retrieve the ladle?"

109

"As long as I can get there before them, everything will work out."

I stared at her. "It will all work out? You're being extremely optimistic."

She shrugged one shoulder, making her breasts jiggle in her tiny sports bra, drawing my attention back to a place I was trying to stop thinking about.

"It's worked for me so far." She looked sullen.

"Let me come with you." The words came out of my mouth before I could think. She opened her mouth to protest, and I felt like complaining myself. I had taken bodyguard assignments in the military before, and I was excellent at it. But this task would be different. For one thing, there would be no backup.

I started to justify myself instead of backing down. "We will be together. If anyone investigates the validity of our marriage, they'll see we have been hanging out the whole time." It was true. We didn't have to stay with each other on my planet. She stared at me, shaking her head. On impulse, I added, "We'll tell people we're on our honeymoon."

Even though it might not be the smartest decision, I didn't want to let Emmy go. I knew I might never see her again. An uncertain future stretched in front of her. She didn't realize how quickly people could have their lives ended. But I did. I had seen plenty of death.

I didn't want Emmy to die. I wanted her to live so I could get to know more about her. She was a puzzle I needed to solve. I wasn't going to have a chance if she were light-years away from me.

Besides, I didn't feel like going home just to sit in my big empty house again. The prospect of adventure called to me just as much as Emmy did. Hadn't I been saying I was bored with my life? I didn't want to lose all the money I inherited and the lifestyle that went with it, of course. But I also wanted something more than merely spending it.

"I can't let you do that," she said.

I was surprised at how disappointed I felt.

"It's not that I don't want you to come."

"Well, what is it, then?" I folded my arms across my chest.

"I don't want you to risk your life on something dangerous. It's my life's work, but it's not yours. Go back to your house and your money. That's your specialty and what you want, remember? You wanted it so much you were willing to marry a stranger who's not your type."

When she put it like that, I seem like an asshole. I started getting annoyed that she was pointing out what I already knew about myself but didn't want to acknowledge. She was already challenging me and my self-image. It was bothersome that she remembered a stupid comment I made about her not being my type.

I had wanted some things before, but now things were different.

"I don't know who you think I am, but you don't have to worry about me. I can handle whatever is coming our way on your impossible mission."

* * *

EMMY

"Excuse me?" I asked. "These guys, they aren't archeologists. They're treasure hunters. More like upscale criminals. They don't play by the same rules I do. They mean business and I don't think you knows what that means."

"That's where you're wrong, Emmy."

"Could you explain yourself?" I said, feeling frustrated. How could this man make me feel so many emotions in the space of a few minutes?

The sounds of people bumping around were getting louder, but nobody had come into the cargo hold yet.

"I'm ex-military."

"Oh." That explained the shot on the car to destroy their batteries. I wondered if he was the sexy kind of ex-military, or an accountant or a chef. I didn't want to ask.

112

"I could help you. I could make sure those guys don't interfere with getting Zelia's ladle."

I felt myself wavering. The task would be less daunting if I had a partner.

But was that selfish? Just because something was hard to do alone didn't mean I should automatically accept Ven's help, no matter how trained he was.

I shook my head, my chest beginning to choke with regret.

"I'm sorry, Ven. It's not your problem. I couldn't possibly accept your help."

"Maybe your problem is that you try to do everything yourself." His eyes looked like black pools in the semi-darkness.

I froze. He had no right to call me out on something like that. He wasn't my friend, and he was barely my husband. Although...

He was probably correct.

Even so, he couldn't come with me. "It's not going to happen, Ven. I promise I'll return after I get the ladle. I'll be your wife for a year so you can keep your money."

"What if you don't come back because you can't?" He had a thoughtful look on his face. I felt a stab of fear. Could I die out there?

"Then you won't have to fake my death because I'll actually be dead. I'll send proof that I'm on an assignment for work. You won't have any trouble with people thinking I left you."

He was shaking his head and about to say something else when the spaceship started moving.

Ven went to the small port window and looked out. "It sounds like we're taking off."

"Into space? We're going to die together, I guess." I tasted fear for what seemed like the hundredth time today.

"Strap in." He grabbed my hand and pulled me to a seat. "We're leaving."

"Don't we need to know where we're going first?"

"I have no idea. If you don't want to be a pancake when we get there, fasten your restraints."

At least I was getting away from Stalwart.

CHAPTER 13

VEN

I felt the shuttle touch down on an unknown planet. An announcement sounded and seemed to be giving instructions for getting off the spacecraft. I didn't know for sure because they weren't speaking Standard. Emmy nodded like she understood every word.

Of course she could speak the language. What other secrets lay hidden inside her head? I felt a tightening in my gut, and an old feeling of inadequacy threaten to overtake me. Was I smart enough or good enough to be here? My mind knew it wasn't true, but I couldn't control my body's reactions.

"I'm surprised you can understand that." I tried to distract myself from my feelings.

She had the decency to blush. "I guess it's strange that I know a few extra languages. Morley made me learn it because he thought it might be useful. He also encouraged me to learn English."

"English?" Merely saying the word made my mouth feel peculiar.

"It's one of the ancient languages from Earth. It's an irrelevant but interesting factoid about me."

"I supposed it is." I did not want to know any more interesting factoids about Emmy.

Suddenly she looked uncomfortable. "We need to go now."

"Of course," I said, tilting my head and listening. "We're going. We have to be on guard in case someone's waiting for us."

"I meant we have to go right now. I need to use the restroom."

I shook my head. Women.

"Don't give me that look. Just because you have a one-gallon bladder, doesn't mean everyone else does."

"The flight was only a few hours. The ship must have hyperdrive capabilities. There's no way we could have reached another planet this quickly without it. You're lucky it wasn't a three-day flight. I wonder what time it is here."

"Three hours are as endless as three days when nature calls." She started squirming around in her seat.

"Is another interesting factoid that you're a bad poet? We'll get off, but we can't rush around."

We heard the sounds of several people leaving. "We're on Heralla." I had checked my computer twice to confirm. "Isn't that where you wanted to go? Where the ladle is?"

"Zelia's ladle. And yes, it is."

"That can't be a coincidence."

116

"Something doesn't seem right," she agreed, looking troubled.

"It's close to sundown. We should wait until it's dark to leave the ship, but I suppose it won't hurt to take a peek."

"What if it's a trap?"

I held up my gun. "Then they will get an unpleasant surprise."

In about a minute, the ship was quiet. It was time to move. "Okay, let's go." I opened the door. "Stay close to me."

Emmy followed as we crept through the dark cargo hold to the door. I opened it quietly and surveyed the hallway, trying to see if there was anyone around.

It was empty.

I stepped out into the corridor. There was no sign of people. The ship was silent. We could hear voices outside, but we would worry about them later.

"Finally. A bathroom." Emmy spotted the sign on one of the doors. "I have to go." She ducked into the room before I could stop her.

She wouldn't be able to run if her bladder was about to burst. Come to think of it, neither would I.

I took my turn and with both of us feeling relieved, we made our way to the exit of the spaceship. I stopped at one of the windows and gazed outside, studying the people milling around.

Our shuttle wasn't far from the main building, which was good. The sooner we could mix in with everyone else, the better. As I watched the people, I heard Emmy come up behind me. She cursed when she looked out the window.

"We didn't end up on Heralla accidentally. Abel's men knew we were on the ship. They brought us here on purpose."

I turned to look at her. "How could you know that?"

She drew in a deep breath. I could see she was scared. "The guy out there with the white hair is Abel. He makes coincidences happen."

I looked out the window. There was a person outside with long white hair which fluttered in the wind. He seemed stick-thin and frail, like an elderly man. As I watched, he indicated where his people should put the supplies, slightly tottering as he ordered them around.

"What are the chances that we stowed away on the ship of the people who were trying to kidnap us?" I asked, mildly amazed.

"Slim to none," she said. "But Abel's powerful and wealthy. Things like this always happen when he's involved."

"They brought us here somehow?"

"I think so." She thought for a moment. "Does it matter how they did it? We shouldn't waste energy trying to figure it out. We're stuck here now, no matter what."

"No, it doesn't," I agreed. "We're where we need to be. It seems like they plan on keeping us here until we can help them find the ladle."

"Zelia's ladle," she corrected me. "You're right. They won't kill me until they get it. They can kill you at any time, although with Abel here they might show some restraint. He doesn't like violence. He just wants to get stuff."

"We need a plan." I looked out the window, watching people come and go. They were unloading climbing equipment and other supplies.

"That looks like some gear to go mountain climbing." She nodded, keeping her eyes on the people outside.

"Yep. The Mestolo's at the top of a mountain."

"How do they know?"

"They got that far before. They stopped when Morley discovered them and turned back. He wasn't going to lead them directly to the artifact. His last transmission came from the top of that mountain," she said, nodding her head to the left. "Before the cave-in."

I shifted my neck and spotted the biggest mountain I had ever seen. It wasn't a place for climbing. It was a place where people died, leaving their corpses frozen for eternity.

"We have to climb that?" I whispered, turning to give Emmy a disgruntled look. She didn't say anything and just looked at me with her big brown eyes. "With Abel's men after us?"

"It will give us the motivation to move quickly."

I smiled for the first time in a long while. Emmy smiled back, and her eyes lit up. She looked fantastic.

I struggled to keep up my end of the conversation, with half of my mind thinking about how beautiful she looked when she smiled. The other half wondered if Emmy had what it took to get up the mountain.

"Definitely motivating. Er…are you sure you'll be able to manage it?" I said, knowing the question would get me in trouble before it was out of my mouth.

"I'll manage just fine. It's you I'm worried about," she said with sincerity.

The nerve of the little wench. "I hope you can keep up with me."

* * *

EMMY

We waited until sundown to get off the spaceship. As the second sun dropped below the horizon, Ven touched my arm, making me jump.

"It looks like there's no one around anymore. Darkness will give us the cover we need to get away. If there's still someone out there guarding the shuttle, we'll have to deal with them. We're not going to get a better chance."

"One more thing," I added. "We can't let them get a head start. If we get onto the mountain ahead of them, we'll be able to move faster because there are only two of us."

"Right. Keep alert." Ven pulled out his gun. He set it to the highest stun setting before lethal. It made me feel nervous and safe at the same time. I was still trying to come to grips with the fact that Ven might be a very dangerous person. He had said he was ex-military. Even if he was bad at his job, he had a lot of training on how to kill people.

I suspected Ven had been an excellent soldier. Once he informed me about his background, I sensed a subtle change in his demeanor. He had given himself permission to act naturally again. When I first met him, I thought he was one of the most mild-mannered guys I had ever seen. Now there was a glint in his eye of pure steel. His face was a mask of concentration.

I knew he could protect me, but I wasn't sure I could do the same for him. If anything happened to him because he helped me, I would never forgive myself.

I followed Ven down a ramp onto the ground and looked around. There was nobody here. At the other end of the spaceport's broad landing pad, there was some activity. A new shuttle was landing. But in our area, the spaceships were all shut down. Their lights were off. Maybe they were left there for the night, or we were in long-term parking. I had no idea.

Jogging lightly across the lot, Ven and I kept to the shadows. As we approached the building, Ven called for a stop on the outside of the circle of lights, giving him a chance to observe the entrance. Heralla was a low-technology planet and had inadequate security. It didn't have people or credits, but it was creating a name for itself as a vacation destination. With its rugged landscape and low population density, it was perfect for people who wanted to get away from urban living.

Even though Heralla had established itself as a wilderness environment, that didn't mean there weren't people here. They congregated in one place, the capital city. It had a population of over seventy million inhabitants, with plenty of culture and interesting things to do.

I had done a lot of research on this planet.

Other than the one city, the rest of the planet held only small towns and vast tracts of wild areas. The last time I was here, I contracted an illness that sent me home. It took me a long time to recover, but I came away with immunity to the disease.

I started making a list in my head of what we needed to do. First, we had to get into the city. That shouldn't be difficult. It was only a twenty-minute hovercraft ride away. After we reached the city, our destination was City Hall, the oldest building on the planet. I hoped to find more information about the Stone Goddess before heading up the mountain.

Morley had given me bits and pieces of information when I talked to him, but he had been too paranoid to send everything at once. He thought Abel's men might be monitoring our conversations. It didn't matter how many layers of encryption he added to our transmissions. He was always worried. He believed if one mind could figure out how to tangle something, another mind could learn how to untangle it.

He gave me all the clues he had, but I would have to figure out a good deal of it by myself. Morley preferred to leave secrets lost to time and hidden away rather than have them uncovered and fall into the wrong hands.

I tried not to think about Morley any longer. But being here brought back all sorts of memories. I returned to my list. Once I had the info that would get us to Zelia's ladle, we would need to get equipment to climb the mountain and buy supplies for the two-day trek.

We need transportation to the base of the mountain. I hoped the entrance to the cave leading to the ladle was at the top.

Once inside, my wits would be the only thing allowing us to find Zelia's ladle. I hoped I was smart enough.

Someone pressed cold metal against my temple. A familiar voice whispered into my ear. "What do we have here?" It was the blond man who had tried to kidnap me on Stalwart. "I believe we have unfinished business, woman."

His hand came around my waist, pulling my body against him so I could feel his hard cock. I pressed my lips together in disgust but didn't move. It would only take a flick of his finger to kill me.

"Put your hands in the air." He directed his command at Ven, who obeyed but watched closely.

"You and I are going to have some fun together before I bring you back. The boss is going to be happy I didn't let you get away." He roughly squeezed my breasts. In the darkness, I wondered if Ven could see what he was doing. "I'm happy myself."

I cut my eyes over to Ven without moving my head. He was glowering and looked like he was ready to jump my assailant.

"Hey man, stand back." The blond man pressed the gun more firmly against my head. "Unless you want her in a coma."

Before he had finished speaking, Ven lunged at us and the gun went off.

CHAPTER 14

VEN

For someone who likes to think of himself as a smart guy, that was a dumb thing to do.

Emmy slumped to the ground as I punched the man hard across the cheek. In broad daylight, he could have seen my attack coming from a mile away, but the darkness concealed the blow. The man cursed and levelled his weapon at me. I had already moved into a different position. He looked around trying to locate me when I landed on his back and tackled him.

I was able to knock the wind out of him. He grabbed onto my body and rolled, ending up on top of me. He managed to throw a few wild punches before I pushed him off and got on my feet again. He was a better fighter than I had expected and powerful, but his size made him slow. I was confident that my training would give me an advantage.

My confidence began to wane when he managed to land some hits on my body. He faked a low attack, making me drop my guard, then hit me with a hard hook to the ear. I fell to the ground, a ringing sound blocking out all the other noises and pain exploding through my head.

Fuck, that hurt.

I had made the classic blunder of underestimating my opponent. Now I was in a fight I might lose, and I couldn't do anything about it. I tried to get up but felt dizzy. The guy took the opportunity to kick me. I groaned as he started taking out all his repressed anger on me, swinging his foot viciously at my stomach.

Without warning, he dropped on his back beside me. Emmy had started fighting back. I sat up just as Emmy delivered a blow to his jawbone, directly between the ear and the chin. The thug fell to the ground and didn't get up again.

"Are you feeling okay?" She reached down and grabbed my hand, helping me to stand.

I felt my ribs. I didn't think he broke them, but I would have some severe bruises. I hoped he hadn't done any damage to my internal organs with those kicks.

"I'll be fine. Let's get out of here. He might be only stunned."

"We have a few minutes. I doubt he'll be getting up soon."

She hooked her arm through mine, making it look like we were a couple on a stroll. Our positioning allowed her to support some of my weight. I was still dizzy from the blow to the ear.

"Speaking of stunned..." The bright lights of the spaceport made us both squint as we entered the building. I winced at the falsely conversational tone of voice. "Why did you move when he told you explicitly to remain where you were? He fucking shot me! I could be in a coma or dead right now."

We passed an older man. Emmy gave him a charming smile and then turned back to me, her eyes shooting daggers.

"I could see the settings on the gun and knew you would only get a brief shock. We needed to get away from him. If anyone catches us, your plan isn't going to work." I looked away from her because I didn't want her to see through my explanation.

"That's bullshit." Her voice sounded furious. "You were angry and wanted a piece of his ass."

"Maybe."

We walked out the main door and found a self-driving hovercraft. After we entered the vehicle, I finally allowed myself to relax, ignoring the pain in my head and my side.

Emmy programmed a destination into the hovercraft, then turned to face me again. "Maybe? That was a bone-headed move. You could have gotten me killed." She paused. "I suppose you could have gotten yourself killed as well."

"I thought I was getting us out of trouble." I didn't like the feeling creeping up on me. Had I made the wrong decision? I preferred it when people didn't question my choices.

"What would you have done if I hadn't knocked him out?"

I didn't have an answer for her.

She answered the question herself. "It's simple. You would have been beaten to within an inch of your life, and you would have screwed up everything."

We lapsed into silence for the rest of the ride. As we pulled to a stop on the corner of a busy street and got out, she put my hand on my arm. I looked down at Emmy's hand briefly, then up at her eyes.

"Promise me you won't do anything stupid. We can figure things out together."

"Did you just ask me to be your partner? I was under the impression that you didn't need any help." I didn't bother to disguise the bitterness in my voice.

"I understand I need help now." I felt my eyebrows go up in surprise. "But I'll never need the kind that's going to get us both killed."

"Fine." I knew I wasn't being graceful, but it was the best I could do. "I won't do anything stupid, and we'll make decisions as a team."

"Great. Let's never talk about it again. I know someone who owes me a favor."

* * *

I couldn't stand this woman anymore. I was following her down an alley in the middle of the city, and I was seething. She had called me stupid twice. I regretted coming along on her ridiculous suicide mission, and I could not believe that she had given me shit for trying to save her ass.

What annoyed me most was the idea that she might be right. It had been an ill-advised move and one I would never have usually made. When he started talking about doing things to Emmy, his words had driven me over the edge.

Was I supposed to stand there and listen to him? I saw red and jumped into action. I put my hand to my forehead as I finally calmed down and realized what an incredibly dumb thing I had done.

And that was when I finally understood. In general, I was intelligent, but I had made a mistake. Making the occasional silly decision didn't mean I was worthless.

Sometimes everyone was stupid, and it didn't matter in the long run. I didn't need to let my feelings control me anymore. The world wasn't going to end. In fact, it might be good that Emmy was smarter than me. If I did something idiotic, she could bail me out.

I stared at the dirty wall of the building as she pressed her thumb against a small square on the wall. A screen lit up with the words *Please Wait*.

All this time I had tried to run away from situations questioning my intelligence. I made sure to get a good job, never be caught flat-footed, and fill my head with knowledge, all so I would never have to feel dumb. In one shattering moment, my sense of self-worth was changing.

I gazed at Emmy, feeling grateful. She would never know what she had done to set me free. "What is it?" She had noticed me looking at her.

"Nothing." I flashed my best smile, liking the way she blushed and dropped her gaze. We were still waiting as we heard the sounds of someone moving around on the other side of the door. "What's taking so long?"

"Morley warned me this person is extremely paranoid. I'm not sure what kind of security he has in place. He might be moving all the furniture away from the front door."

"Who exactly are we going to see? Are you sure you can trust him?" I folded my arms across my chest. Emmy unconsciously emulated my position, holding her arms across her front and making her breasts compress together. It had been hot all day, but now that the suns had set, it was getting cold. I could see goosebumps pebbled across her skin. We both needed a shower and a change of clothes.

I hoped our host could offer us that much.

The thought of her taking a shower was distracting. I tried to concentrate on the task at hand, rather than how her soft naked body would feel pressed up against mine as warm water dripped over our bodies. She was answering my question, and I tried to pay attention while the blood rushed out of my brain, heading south.

"His name is David. Morley said I could trust him completely."

"And you believe him?"

"He was never wrong." She acted like that was enough to explain everything.

I had never met either one of these men. I wasn't trusting anyone until they proved themselves. We needed help before we continued on our way, but I wouldn't let him out of my sight around Emmy.

I wondered why I felt overly protective. I supposed it was because she was my wife, whether in name only or not. She was my responsibility. I would take care of her to the best of my ability.

The door finally opened, revealing a withered old face which scrutinized us. Apparently he hadn't felt the need to enhance his physical appearance as he aged. I had never seen that many wrinkles before.

"What do you want?" His furry eyebrows drew together.

"Are you David?" Emmy said. "Morley sent me."

"Morley? It's too late for him to send you anywhere. A cave-in collapsed on him. He's dead, honey."

David didn't attempt to soften his words. My heart ached as I saw Emmy's eyes fill with tears.

"I know. He was my friend. He said you could help me."

The man shrugged as if he didn't care. "Fine. Come in and tell me your story."

Emmy smiled and stepped through the door. I followed her closely. She might believe David, but there was something fishy about him. I didn't trust him at all.

CHAPTER 15

VEN

I hovered behind Emmy like a storm cloud as we followed David into the room beyond the alleyway. I don't know what I had expected. Perhaps a dirty kitchen with stained walls and dirty floors. I had not imagined a full-blown forensics laboratory. Emmy looked around in wonder.

"What is this place?" I asked.

"It's a dream come true." She wasn't looking at me, but she had a big smile on her face. "I've always wanted a state-of-the-art archeology lab."

The room was painted a crisp white and filled with counters and tables. There were screens and computers, as well as storage — hundreds of narrow shelves filled with trays containing bits of dirt and pottery.

"It's the place where Morley brought his treasures for analysis," David remarked.

"Really? I've always wondered what happened after we found an artifact." Emmy looked around the room intently. "This is where Morley would take the most valuable pieces after we had a big find? He must have come here to examine the artifacts in a sterile environment. I wonder why he never told me."

The man's thin silver hair lightly floated as he nodded his head.

"I wouldn't let him. The laboratory is the city's best-kept secret. Morley knew that there were other things to find here on Heralla." The man turned to me and began to lecture. I didn't come here to be treated like a student, but I tried to listen, knowing that it might be important to Emmy. "There was once a thriving civilization on this planet, founded by some of the best minds of the Great Race. There was a disaster and most of their inventions were lost forever."

He was silent for a moment, thinking about the past.

"Fortunately for us, not all of their knowledge disappeared. Their scientists saved some and hid it for future generations. They used puzzles to conceal information, ensuring only worthy people would be able to find it. They hid the artifacts but left clues pointing to their location."

"So where are these clues?" I asked.

Emmy was thinking carefully, her whole being focused on the strange old man.

"An ancient order of monks existed on Heralla for thousands of years before the Great Race discovered the planet. They received some of the secrets."

"Wait a minute. How do you know this?" Emmy's tone of voice sounded suspicious. "Morley said that I was the only other one who knew about these things."

She broke off her thoughts, and I realized she had stopped herself from mentioning the ladle.

"Morley was correct." The old man stared into Emmy's eyes with unrelenting fervor. I stepped closer to her. It was hard to tell the difference between enthusiasm and insanity.

"Look, I can do the math. If I know and you know, that's three people."

She stopped speaking and looked at David carefully, tilting her head and examining him as if she was trying to unlock a secret. Emmy said something in a foreign language. It sounded like it hissing snakes and sharp poking sounds.

David answered in the same language.

I looked back and forth between the two, hoping I could learn an entirely new language without training and by observation. The foreign tongue was only the beginning of my problems. The next thing I knew, his face started melting away.

* * *

EMMY

From the moment David opened the door, something felt wrong. Morley said I could trust him, but something made me feel very uncomfortable.

135

I couldn't shake the feeling as we walked in and he revealed an amazing research facility. I was instantly jealous of David. If Morley and I had access to a place like this over the years, things would have been different. We could have preserved more of the excavations.

The more he talked, the more my sense of unease increased. The last straw was when he mentioned the monks. Morley and I were the only ones who knew about those puzzle-loving monks. Had he forced Morley to tell him? Or was it something it else?

I decided to try something in English. "The tide holds the knowledge, the highs and lows."

"Time is a portal, as it ebbs and flows."

"How do you know that verse?" I asked.

He didn't answer me directly. Instead, he gazed at me with eyes that suddenly seemed as familiar as my own.

"Don't take this the wrong way." I hesitated. My breath started to come unevenly. "You're supposed to be dead."

"Emmy, it would take more than a cave-in to kill me."

He reached into his pocket, pulling out a small remote control. David's false face melted away. It must have been a creation of holographic technology. When the disguise disappeared, I saw Morley standing and beaming at me.

Morley was a tall man. He had never revealed his exact age, but I knew he was probably in his sixties. His silver-gray hair was still quite thick, and the bright blue eyes that I had missed so much were dancing. I couldn't believe he was here. I had wished many times for a moment like this and the opportunity to see him again.

"Morley!" I yelled, throwing myself into his arms. "You're alive!"

He hugged me tightly and stepped back to look at me. "The last time I saw you, I wasn't sure if I would ever see you again."

"They said you were dead."

"Missing and presumed dead," he clarified. "They presumed wrong. I had to get away from Abel's men somehow. When the roof of the cave came crashing down, and I knew I had a back way out, the solution seemed obvious. I couldn't ask for a better opportunity to fake my death."

I looked at him in disbelief. "You put me through hell. You know that, right?"

"I'm sorry, dear. It was all for Zelia's ladle. You know that." He put his hand on my shoulder. The hint of an apology shone in his eyes.

Ven cleared his throat and spoke in Standard. "Are you going to tell me who this person is, Emmy?" He was trying to keep himself under control.

"Of course. Ven, this is Morley. He's been hiding from Abel's men so they couldn't get any information about Zelia's ladle from him." I hesitated until Ven started glowering at me. "Morley, this is my husband, Ven."

Morley's eyes nearly bugged out of his head. "You told me you weren't going to get married. You said your work was everything."

I heard a hint of disappointment in his voice. I wasn't surprised. I was disappointed in myself.

"It wasn't on purpose. I was helping out a friend." I glanced at Ven quickly. I wondered if I would be in trouble when we were alone again, but I didn't care. Morley was alive! He would fix everything.

"How is this possible?" He gave me a stern look. "I'm sure this story is fascinating."

"It's about as interesting as a dead man returning to life. I was running away from Abel's men. They tracked me to Earth. I went to the spaceport hoping to get a ticket off-planet, but everything was sold out." I glanced at Ven, but his expression was unreadable. "I met a woman there. A beautiful, tall, thin blonde woman."

The excessive description was for Ven's benefit.

"I begged her to let me exchange her ticket."

"Why would she agree to something like that?"

"Well, I had to sweeten the deal. I offered her the entire 500,000 credits you gave me to pay for the trip back here."

Ven's eyebrows drew together. I realized this was the first time I mentioned a payment. Did he think his chosen bride was a saint who would help someone because she was a good person? If that was true, he had been a poor judge of character.

Morley nodded then. "That makes more sense."

Ven still looked upset. "She wouldn't help you out of the goodness of her heart without payment?"

I shrugged. "Money makes the world go around. We're not all independently wealthy. I didn't think much of it at the time. I could have been trying to swindle her out of her ticket, you know."

"She didn't have to take that much. You gave her more than the cost of the ticket."

I looked at him with compassion. That naive alien must have thought Montana was something special.

"She was Ven's perfectly chosen woman, but he ended up with me instead."

"So you just whoever walked off the spaceship instead of the other woman?" I knew Morley was trying not to be judgemental, but he was failing.

139

"It's not as bad as it sounds." I surprised myself by defending Ven. "He needed to get married so he could keep an inheritance from his uncle."

That was possibly the worst thing I could have said. Morley quietly stared at me. As always, his silence said more than his words.

"I meant what I said when I married Emmy." Ven said took a step and stood beside me. "I promised I would protect her and take care of her. I'm doing that now, to the best of my ability. I wouldn't let her come here alone." He positioned himself so his arm touched mine. He didn't have the courage to put his arm around me, though I imagined he wanted to. "She wanted to face everything alone."

Morley nodded. "Emmy can take care of herself."

"With all due respect, sir, everyone needs some help sometimes."

There was a pause while we waited for Morley's evaluation of Ven. We waited in vain. Morley tended to delay his judgment until he had all the information.

"Well, we shall see what will come of it." His words sounded mild, but I knew there was a challenge behind them.

I looked back and forth between the two men, wondering if they had finished their testosterone show. I had more important things to do.

"You two had better get showered and dressed. You've got a ball to attend," Morley said, patting me on the back.

"I do?"

"It's time to play Cinderella, Emmy." Morley had a grin on his face. I didn't know what he had in mind, but I had a feeling I wasn't going to like it.

* * *

We were walking quickly through the streets. I tried not to stumble in the lovely but impractical shoes Morley insisted I wear. Ven was parking the hovercraft as close as he could in case we needed to leave in a hurry.

"When I got to the cave and saw the mirror and the riddle, they looked familiar. I noticed they were almost identical to the ones at City Hall. A clue to Zelia's ladle has to be with the mirror. The mirror and the riddle are connected somehow. We just have to figure it out."

I nodded again. We had been over this three times already. I tried to change the subject, knowing he was getting anxious because he couldn't help himself.

"The festival of the Stone Goddess lasts for a week. We're lucky we arrived in time for the final day of celebrations," I said.

Morley nodded. "It's fortunate, but there's no such thing as fate. Everything happens for a reason."

"Fate has definitely taken a hand in all this," I said, thinking about Ven.

"Do you love him?" Morley sounded more curious than anything.

"No," I said. "Of course not."

My mind drifted back to our kiss. But that was lust, not love.

"Methinks the lady doth protest too much."

"Not Shakespeare. It was bad enough you made me read it when I was learning English. I shouldn't be subjected to it now. Just because everyone says he's good doesn't make him good."

"The Bard is one of Earth's greatest artists, and you should have more respect for his work. Emmy, do you have feelings for this man? He's an alien, for heaven's sake. Why would you marry him?"

"I told you the truth, Morley. I needed to get away from Abel's men at the time, so I said I would go with him. When I learned his entire tale of woe, I felt bad because I had stolen his bride away from him. I was trying to fix a mistake."

I looked away from Morley's gaze quickly, worried that he might see something concealed in my heart. I didn't love Ven, so I didn't think he would discover a hidden secret. But Morley was always able to penetrate my thoughts, and I wanted some privacy right now.

"I'm worried about you, Emmy. Marriage isn't something to be taken lightly."

"I'm giving the marriage the full consideration it deserves."

Morley paused for a moment, then blurted out a thought. "Perhaps Ven should not be part of our search. How much do we know about him? Can he be trusted with these secrets?"

I bristled at the thought. "Ven saved my life at great personal risk. He left a comfortable home and came with me. We can trust him." I was feeling indignant.

"That speaks of a strong commitment," Morely observed. "In fact, it's a surprising amount of effort from one stranger to another."

"We're not strangers."

"Are you sure?"

"We're husband and wife."

"In all ways?" he whispered. He wanted to know if I had slept with Ven.

"I don't think that's any of your business. I trust him, Morley. You will too."

"Very well. I will defer to your judgment, but I will form my opinion of the young man and whether he is good enough for you."

I smiled at him and he kissed me on the cheek.

"Now it's time for Cinderella to go to the ball."

"Do I have to, Morley? Isn't there another way to get in?"

"Not during the festival of the Stone Goddess. You know how these people are. When everyone is drunk and exhausted from their reveling, you will have an opportunity to slip away. The mirror is the key to the ladle. Tonight we're counting on you and your brain."

"Okay." I suddenly felt nervous. "Be ready in case I need any help."

"Of course I'll be prepared, but I don't think you'll need to contact me."

I huffed out my breath, feeling more anxious than ever.

"You can do this, Emmy. I have great faith in you."

"Are you sure you can't come with me?"

"The scanners would see right through my holographic face. Morley must remain dead. You see that, don't you? Once the truth came out, Abel would know about it immediately."

"I guess you're right, but I wish things were different. We could be partners again."

"Perhaps it's time for you to get a new partner," he said under his breath. Ven walked up after parking the

144

hovercraft. I stared at the sight of him impeccably dressed in formal attire. He looked unbelievably handsome. My heart started to pound in my chest. Ven walked toward me like a magnet was pulling him. With a visible effort, he turned his head and greeted Morley, then returned his gaze to my face.

"You look beautiful." His eyes locked onto mine.

"So do you." I felt tongue-tied and wished I could think of something more interesting to say.

"I'll let you two get to work," Morley said. He had a smile on his face that went completely over my head. I was flabbergasted by Ven's appearance. "Contact me if you have any emergencies."

Ven held out his arm to me. I took it, and my pulse raced. I had never felt this way before. It was like I might float away at any moment.

"Are you ready?" He flashed a smile that made my body perk up and take notice.

"I am if you are." I was ready for anything.

He led me to the front of the building where destiny waited for us.

CHAPTER 16

VEN

I glided into the large ballroom after we passed through security, feeling like my feet were barely touching the floor. The way Emmy had looked before we entered the room dramatically affected me. My heart was still pounding from the heat in her eyes.

She came off like a dream, wearing a long dress that swept the floor. The bodice was tight around her chest, putting her large breasts on display. The rest of the dress curved over her sensual hips on its way to the ground. She was turning me on so much that I had to focus my attention elsewhere so I wouldn't embarrass myself.

I had never been attracted to a curvy woman before. The tall, slender women from my dating history were usually thin. No hips, no butts, and small breasts. I had slept with plenty and enjoyed every moment.

But now that I had Emmy on my arm, I was beginning to wonder what I had ever seen in those types of women in the first place. The dress hugged her luscious curves in a way I didn't know I desired until I saw it. I wasn't the only one who noticed. She was turning male heads all over the place as we walked through the packed room.

The atmosphere was romantic. Music filled the dimly-lit ballroom. People held drink glasses as big as bowls and drained them as quickly as possible. Lavish furnishings and luxurious decor packed every corner.

146

She stopped before an ancient stone wheel on display in the main party room.

"Do you know the history of this object too?"

Emmy barely heard me. She looked entranced and put her hand on the glass case as if she wanted to touch the smooth stone. "It's a depiction of the Stone Goddess. She's always shown as a wheel that has no beginning and no end."

I wasn't impressed.

She read a placard describing the artifact. *"The Stone Goddess leaves no survivors.* I'm not sure what it means, but I bet we get a chance to find out." She gave me a dazzling smile. "The Stone Goddess is tomorrow's problem. We should dance now." She reached out her hand and pulled me onto the dance floor.

"We'll be able to see more this way," she whispered. "Move me around the room."

I was happy to hold her in my arms. I took her hand, lowering my arm around her waist. When I pulled her body next to me, I knew I didn't want a wealthy but boring life any longer. It had been fun for a while, and nice having anything I wanted. But that life was ultimately meaningless. I wanted something and someone more. The person I wanted was in my arms right now. I glanced down at Emmy, who was dazzled either by the opulence or my proximity.

"Emmy." I wasn't sure how to express the words in my heart.

"Yes?" Her voice sounded strangled. I wondered again if she was affected by my presence as I was by hers. She had enjoyed our stolen kiss on the spaceship, but I told her we were going to remain friends.

"Do you remember what I said after we kissed?" Her breathing quickened.

"Of course. Our relationship will be strictly platonic. If I wanted you..." She hesitated, her skin turning a delicate pink as her voice dropped lower. "...in my bed, I would have to make the first move. Why? Do you want me to change my mind?"

"I'm just making sure you remembered."

She looked troubled by my words, but I had a feeling that she was getting to the point where her desire for me would outweigh her objections. She was holding onto her ideals because she was scared.

To be honest, she wasn't the only one. The possibility of falling in love with Emmy was disturbing. I wasn't ready for the level of truth required in such a relationship.

But whenever I stared into Emmy's soft brown eyes, I knew I couldn't simply let her go, either.

Wasn't I a brave man? A soldier? If I could risk my life in battle, why couldn't I risk my heart with an Earth woman? Part of me knew an authentic relationship with

Emmy would be more difficult than putting my life on the line. If I made a mistake in battle, at least I was dead and my problems were over.

Her body moved to the music, shifting against mine. I wondered what it would feel like if she moved underneath me as I buried myself into her body.

"What are you thinking?" she whispered. We were dancing close enough for me to feel her nipples against my chest.

I whispered into her ear, making her shiver. "If I told you, it wouldn't be considered polite conversation."

"Where would it be considered polite conversation?" I knew she was out of her depth.

"You'll have to come to my bed if you want to find out."

Maybe she wasn't out of her depth. She ground her body closer to me, making me draw in a quick breath.

"Don't make suggestions if you're not prepared to follow up on them." She put her cheek on my shoulder, but not before I saw her blush.

"I mean it. See me tonight and find out how much."

I heard her swallow, and she shuddered. I smiled in satisfaction. Maybe I would have a midnight visitor, or maybe I wouldn't, but I knew she was interested. It was only a matter of time before she succumbed to the pull between us.

Would she realize we were good together? We hadn't had much time, but there was something about us that instantly clicked. I wondered if fate brought us one another.

"I thought your type was tall, blonde, and skinny." She lifted her head to look me in the eyes. Would I never live that down?

"That was long ago when I was young and dumb. I've changed my type since then."

"Oh?" I heard a spark in her voice. "And what's your type now?"

"Short, curvy, and feisty." I lowered my voice so only she could hear me. "With breasts I could get lost in."

"Stop." She cut me off, and I wondered if I had offended her. When I looked down at her face, I realized she had seen something.

"Look over there." She gestured with her finger. I looked where she was pointing, but didn't see anything important enough to interrupt our sexy banter. Emmy's eyes looked focused, though, and the time for joking had passed.

"That mirror is critical. Let's go check it out."

I strained my neck, but I could barely see it from the ballroom. "Lead on, my lady." I gestured with my hand.

"Don't call me that." Emmy led me across the crowded room. "I'm not a lady."

"Maybe not, but you're going to be mine."

She didn't answer me. I wondered if she had heard me amidst all the noise. I liked the thought of possessing her, but I knew that would come with other problems. If that happened, she would own part of me as well. There was no way for me to gain her heart without losing mine.

"I don't belong to anyone."

She did hear me. I couldn't argue with her, but I wanted to.

It was easy for us to drift off down the hall, ending up in front of the mirror. A volatile mass of dancing and drinking bodies filled the main room. It seemed like the festival of the Stone Goddess celebrated the blessing of Heralla with spirits. The main event consisted of consuming as much alcohol as possible using glasses the size of soup bowls.

People were already stumbling and falling over each other. By morning, the floor would be littered with hungover bodies and smell like sex.

"I think this mirror is over a thousand years old."

"How do you know?"

"It was created for the first queen on Heralla. That statue was made in her image." She pointed to a remarkably life-like bust of a woman on the mantle above the fireplace. "The monks gave the mirror to her as a present. Morley and I researched this planet to death. We know everything an outsider can know about its history."

"If you know everything, then what are we supposed to do now?"

"We had a poem linked to the mirror. On our last attempt, Morley nearly penetrated the monk's outer defenses on the mountain, but he got stuck. He found a cave that was supposed to contain a passage to Zelia's ladle. The only thing in the cave was a mirror, just like this one."

"He made it that far, then gave up and left?" It sounded strange to me.

"Yeah, it's a little odd. But Morley thinks he missed something, and the poem would help us open the gate." Emmy began to recite.

It looks like glass but yet it's not

If you look through an awful lot

Secrets will begin to show

The glass will melt like fallen snow

"It's not the best poetry, but I guess itt doesn't matter for an ancient riddle," I muttered to myself.

"It loses something in the translation."

We both sank into silence.

"What if the mirror is the gate?" Emmy looked around to see if anyone heard her. Tentatively, she reached out to touch it. Her fingers ran along the glass, and Emmy made a sound of frustration.

Solving riddles wasn't my specialty, but this seemed simple enough. All we had to do was follow the directions. "I think you should stand in front of the mirror and look into it."

Emmy shook her head. I could see she thought my solution was too easy. Part of me agreed with her. It probably wouldn't work, but it didn't hurt to try.

She stood in front of the mirror and looked into her reflection. As I watched her face, I saw an almost invisible, thin beam of red light focus on her retina.

"Something is scanning your eye."

She didn't move. "Do you think it's finished?"

"I don't see a laser anymore. Is there anything different about the mirror?"

Emmy reached out her hand slowly, almost reverently, and touched the mirror. Nothing happened. It was still hard glass.

"Perhaps it knows you're not the queen. Would the scan be keyed to the queen's eye?"

"They have to be looking for something. The mirror must be the gate, and we have to figure out how to open it."

She shook her head. "Other people needed access. What if one of the monks wanted to use the ladle? They must have had a way inside."

Emmy looked at the bust of the queen and snatched it up. A light went on and I knew an alarm started ringing somewhere. She ignored the light and came back to the mirror, holding the bust up in front of her face and making the statue look at itself in the mirror. I watched the laser scan the bust's eye. We heard a soft beep and Emmy drew in a sharp breath.

"I hope that worked." She placed the bust back on the mantle and returned to the mirror.

When she reached out to tap it, I expected to hear her fingers rapping on hard glass again. But when she touched the mirror this time, her fingertips went through.

I realized that we might not even be looking at a mirror. Was it a type of sophisticated holographic technology, creating the illusion of a reflection? If so, how was she able to touch it before? And why couldn't she touch it now?

"There's nothing there anymore."

"We don't have time to waste. When you took the bust, it set off an alarm. Abel's men can't be far behind."

"I know." With a smile in my direction, Emmy stepped through the mirror and disappeared.

CHAPTER 17

VEN

Everything about this situation was bizarre. How had monks from thousands of years ago possessed anything remotely similar to modern technology? It might even be a more advanced holographic science than we had now.

I looked around. We were at the top of a curving staircase that descended into darkness. The stepping stones consisted of the same red rock used to construct the building. I pulled out a flashlight.

"Are you ready?" I said to Emmy. Her eyes were lit up like a child opening a present.

"The monks gave the queen the mirror as a gateway into the catacombs. Morley will be surprised."

"Are we supposed to contact Morley? This wasn't part of the plan."

"Maybe." She checked her computer. "We couldn't even if we had to. There's no signal in here. Someone in the rocks here blocks communication. Morley and I had the same problem when we explored some of the tunnels in the mountain."

"I wonder if it makes more sense to go forward or retreat and consult him?"

She frowned. "We were supposed to get information, then return to the mirror in the mountain. But we're close to the ladle already. If we go back out and talk withMorley, we might never get another chance to sneak in again. I think we should go on."

"Are you sure?" I didn't feel as confident as she sounded.

She nodded. "Listen to me." She stepped in front of me on the stairs. "We're going to an ancient place. Monks set up different levels of protection to kill thieves and prevent them from reaching Zelia's ladle."

"Kill?" That was the only word in the sentence that mattered to me. "You're not joking."

"Nope. Morley and I gathered a lot of information about this place. There are at least sixteen different types of booby traps."

I looked down at Emmy's breasts questioningly.

"Not those kind of boobies." She pursed her lips as if she were trying not to smile. "Traps to surprise and kill trespassers. I have an idea of what they look like and which signs mark them, so I'll take the point. Just for your information, there are three that appear to be most common. Pan-jee traps, the spike board, and the door trap."

"Those all sound the same."

"Pan-jee traps are concealed pits with spikes at the bottom, designed to impale you. The spike board is probably self-explanatory."

"And the door trap?"

"More spikes, but these swing down and impaling you when a door opens."

"These monks weren't very creative. You should make body armor part of your official archeologist's outfit. Those are just the major ones?"

"Yes. That's why we think Zelia's ladle is still here. No one's been brave enough to go in and get it. The government of Heralla banned anyone from entering for the past century. They recently lifted the ban, but there hasn't been a mad rush of exploration. Legends about the catacombs have been around for a long time. When we did field research and talked to the locals, they told stories containing unusual traps, like pools of water with globes of cesium inside."

"Let's pretend I don't know anything about Earth chemistry."

"Cesium reacts explosively with water. They also mentioned crossbows."

"At least those are traditional weapons an average person can understand."

"When the first archeologists went inside, guess what they found?"

"Ancient crossbows that crumbled when people looked at them and turned to dust?"

She shook her head, her eyes looking animated as she spoke. "There were fully functional crossbows coated with chromate, which perfectly preserved them."

"I don't believe it."

"One man died when they encountered a pool of water. There wasn't anything over it, but glass spheres containing something volatile filled the water. When he waded through, the glass spheres broke, triggering an explosion which killed him and injured several others. No one has been brave enough to go any further."

"There's a thin line between bravery and stupidity."

She shrugged. "Whatever you want to call it."

"We're going down there?"

"Yes?" She glanced at me. "You can stay here. I don't expect you to risk your life for me, married or not married."

"I don't think I could live with myself if I let you go down there by yourself."

She rubbed her fancy shoe against the stone floor. "Let's go."

"You're not properly dressed, Emmy." I motioned to her fancy dress.

"That's right." She grabbed hold of her skirt and ripped it off. Underneath the dress were beige pants with pockets stuffed with useful things. The top of the dress

159

now looked like a tank top. I noticed her shoes resembled boots from a particular angle. They looked expensive, but they didn't have heels. The footwear looked perfect for trekking through underground passageways dug by monks long ago.

Now wearing clothes befitting an archeological expedition, she stepped down a few of the red stone stairs. She turned back when she realized I wasn't with her.

"What is it?" She looked up at me with concern.

I knew I wouldn't have the right words to express how much she impressed me. "You came prepared."

"It's a habit of mine." Emmy's eyes shone with amusement. "Wearing a dress over a complete archeological dig outfit wasn't my idea, though. It was Morley's creation. Shall we?" She held out her hand.

* * *

EMMY

We reached the bottom of the stairs and crossed into a passageway. As soon as we entered, the hall illuminated itself with a soft glow. I looked around trying to identify the light source, but I couldn't see it.

"Where's the light coming from?"

"I don't know." I shook my head. "The monks had advanced technology like these lights and the mirror. No one knows where it from." I wished I had a better explanation, but I didn't know the answers.

It felt like we walked for about a mile before we encountered the first problem. When we saw a T shape on the floor, Ven and I flattened ourselves against the wall before I tripped it with my toe. A second later, a spike trap popped up, looking vicious and completely functional.

"We would have died." Ven stared at the spikes.

I nodded, not saying a word. We left it activated and continued moving. Soon after we found the first pool with cesium spheres.

"We don't want to trigger this one." We carefully edged around the pool and walked down a passageway. "It would start an enormous explosion."

After the pool, we found ourselves traveling through catacombs which ran under the mountain. It must have taken many years to excavate these tunnels. I heard stories about monks who had gotten lost and never found their way out, walking for miles and never coming to the end. There was supposed to be a cemetery down here, and everything felt creepy.

As we walked along, keeping watch for any obstacles, I felt overwhelmed by different emotions. Excitement about getting to explore these catacombs and anxiety we might be hurt. Ven evoked mixed feelings. Lust, for one, whenever I looked at him. But there was another feeling that was hard to describe. It was a happy feeling that seemed to come from being in his presence.

"Emmy, I want you to know something."

I glanced over at him briefly before returning my eyes to the floor and walls. "You may speak. We're the only people here." I was curious to know what he wanted to tell me. "Wait a minute." I saw something unusual and stopped, putting my hand over his chest. "Something feels wrong."

I scanned the stone floor and the walls trying to identify what caught my attention. There was a thin line in the shape of a rectangle in the grouting between the tiles. It was barely visible. When I crouched down, I saw there was a crack.

"Come on, Emmy. I'm sure it's nothing." Ven was growing impatient.

"There's something between these stones."

"So what?" He stepped forward. "We'll never get anywhere at this pace."

"Wait!" I heard the screech of stone against stone. I grabbed his hand and yanked, falling back onto the floor, Ven crashing by my side.

"Was that necessary?" He stood up, rubbing his hip. He turned to move forward again but stopped when he saw a pit appear in front of us. Metal spikes and a single decaying body lined the bottom of the hole.

Ven froze. I got up and started dusting myself off, trying not to feel smug. When he finally looked at me, he had a sheepish expression on his face.

"It was necessary if you wanted me to save your ass." I heard attitude coming from my voice despite my best efforts.

"Thank you." He looked like he was suppressing his annoyance again. "I owe you."

I shook my head. "We're even. Do you remember what happened on the road? You saved me from being kidnapped by those assholes."

I placed my hand over his. I was amazed at the tingling sensation from touching our skin together and wondered what would happen if I wanted more. "You're in my world now. You should listen to me, as long as you can handle it."

He was about to say something but relented after a moment. "All right. Lead the way."

We slowly started to walk forward with wary eyes. I pointed out markings indicating a trap was coming. To someone who knew the signs, the monks had ways of showing there was danger ahead and how to avoid it.

"Look at these horizontal cuts in the stone." I traced them with my fingers. "They indicate a trap..." I counted the lines. "Twelve paces away, embedded in the floor. If the lines were vertical, they would mean the trap is in the wall."

"How do you know they didn't make random marks to confuse people?"

"They wouldn't want to kill themselves accidentially. People were living here during construction. Not a lot, but enough to guard the place."

"I suppose not." Ven paused, and I immediately stopped as well.

"What is that thing?" He pointed ahead at a dark patch in the floor directly ahead of us.

"I don't know. Come on."

We slowly inched forward, keeping our eyes on the floor. I motioned Ven to sidestep a tile that triggered a trap. Even at our reduced speed, we almost fell into a deep black hole that obstructed the entire passageway, barring our path. I nearly missed it because I was looking too closely at the tiles.

Ven gasped and put his hand out, shoving me back from the edge. If I had taken one more step, it would have meant my death. As I stumbled backward, I landed on the tile I had been trying to avoid. A beam swung down in a deadly arc, aiming deadly spikes at our heads. Ven tackled me to the ground a moment before I would have been impaled. We lay together on the floor. I saw my fear reflected in his eyes.

"See? I am good for something on this trip. Be careful." His eyes didn't leave me as we slowly rose to our feet. I felt stunned at the near miss.

I wanted to tell him that he was good for more than saving my life. Having him here made everything seem possible. Ven gave me confidence. I felt protected with him beside me no matter what dangers we faced.

But I didn't have the words, so I kept my thoughts to myself.

Gazing into the hole in the floor, I felt my first flicker of doubt. According to legend, the monks wanted to make sure the people who found Zelia's ladle were courageous and genuine. Theoretically, individuals who sought it for personal gain would be discouraged if the penalty was death.

I knew it was a test, but I started to question my motives. Did I want the ladle to benefit others, or to boost my ego? I had no idea, and I didn't know what to do.

I gestured at the gaping abyss. "How are we going to get across?"

CHAPTER 18

VEN

"These guys don't fool around." I looked down, trying to see the bottom of the hole. It seemed bottomless.

"You wouldn't either if you had something precious to protect," Emmy said. "Do you think we can swing across?"

She pointed to the trap, which turned down when we approached the hole. Plummeting to our doom wasn't bad enough. Someone wanted to make sure we were impaled and killed twice.

"That doesn't seem safe."

"Stop acting like I'm crazy because I make different decisions than you." Emmy's eyes flashed. She was furious. I guess I thought of her as crazy, but she imagined herself as persistent, inventive, and courageous.

"There's got to be a better way to get across." I started looking around.

"What do you suggest?" She could have sounded sarcastic, but she was sincere. She only wanted to know what I thought.

I thought for a moment. "You said these catacombs had monks living in them, guarding the ladle after they set the traps, right?"

"That's my understanding, yes."

"They must have had a way to get across." An idea flashed into my brain. Excited, I started feeling around the walls and stepping on the floor stones leading up to the hole.

"It's a sound theory." Emmy followed my lead, doing the same thing along the other wall. "What's your degree in?"

In the past, her question would have made me feel like a failure and an idiot. I would have become angry, and either yelled at her or ignored her. But I had no anger attached to my education any longer.

"I was in the military and liked the ground assignments better than sitting in the classroom. I could have gotten a degree, but I didn't."

That was the truth. I made a choice. It wasn't the same as others, but it was the right one for me.

She glanced at me, meeting my eyes. "Have you ever thought about getting your archeology degree? You'd be a great asset."

I laughed.

"I'm serious. You've got the right sort of mind."

"What do you mean? I'm a soldier. All brawn, no brains." I flexed my bicep.

167

"Yeah, right," she said. "You'd be perfect. You're intelligent. You aren't afraid to go into strange places, and you can think through problems."

At that moment, I got lucky and pressed the right place. Stones slid out from the wall, making a narrow path along the left side of the abyss.

"And find answers that weren't obvious. Brilliant. You'd make a great treasure hunter."

No one had ever told me I was smart in this many different ways. When I gazed into her eyes, I could tell she meant her words. It was a revelation. I no longer believed I was stupid, and the woman in front of me thought I was smart, too.

"I thought you said calling someone a treasure hunter was insulting."

"It is, but I wasn't talking about me." She grinned. "Who goes first?"

"I will. If anything happens, I want to bear the brunt of the damage. You have critical information in your head."

She blushed, then frowned. "Don't talk like that, Ven. We're both going to make it out of here alive."

"Sure." I wanted to seem agreeable. She could think whatever she wanted, but her ideas might not match up to reality. I had gone on missions where the team thought everyone would come out alive. I had been lucky before, but you never knew when your number was up.

I wondered if I would die protecting Emmy. It wouldn't be the worst way to go.

I gingerly put some of my weight on the first stone, testing to see if it would hold before committing my body. I slid my foot over, keeping my back pressed against the wall. I didn't look down. The stones seemed stable, but I wanted to be careful. The first three rocks held, but the fourth one fell into the abyss. I paused for a moment as my heart pounded in my chest. I had to reassure myself that I hadn't dropped with the stone.

Emmy and I locked eyes as we listened for the sound of the rock hitting the floor. I strained my ears for almost a minute but heard nothing.

The next challenge was maneuvering over the gap where the stone had fallen. I felt myself begin to lose my balance and frantically grabbed at anything that would keep me upright. I slowly moved my right foot past the gap. No more stones were damaged. I made the rest of the journey across without incident.

When I reached the other side, I felt a profound sense of relief but tried not to show it. I didn't want Emmy to know how nervous I was even though it would be difficult to hide anything from her. She seemed to see through me already, and her mind penetrated directly into my soul.

Her passage across the narrow path was nerve-wracking. My trip was difficult, but at least I was in control of my destiny. When she reached my side safely, I immediately pulled her into my arms. She clung to me, gripping me as tightly as I was holding her. Then she pulled back and gazed into my eyes.

"Don't worry. I'm right here," she said.

I closed my eyes, and drew in a deep breath, placing a single reverent kiss on her forehead. She bit her lip.

"Come on." She cautiously moved forward. "The fun's just getting started."

* * *

EMMY

When we arrived at the guard's room, I felt like sinking onto the bed and going straight to sleep. I was exhausted. I didn't know if it was because of the longer day on Heralla or all the activity. I had started by leaving Ven's house in the middle of the night. The chase happened in the afternoon. We had arrived on Heralla in the early evening, and the party started at eight at night, Earth time. It felt like past two o'clock in the morning for me.

I had been awake for over twenty hours. I wasn't sure I could keep my eyes open for much longer. Ven didn't seem to be doing much better. For the past hour, we had been triggering each other's yawns.

"Is this place safe?"

I shook my head. I wished it was. "This room is vulnerable to attack. There's something the matter with it. Another place exists and it might even be accessible through this one."

"That makes sense. How do we get to it?"

"Who knows?" I was too tired to think. "Whoever constructed this room was clever and had a lot of time on their hands to think of new ways to make my life difficult." I yawned and covered my mouth. My eyes were watering.

Ven walked around the room, picking up objects and pushing random spots on the wall. "Do you have any idea what I should be looking for?"

"It's probably a pull trigger. You tug on something in the room, and it opens a rotating door."

He tentatively lifted a lamp. "Isn't it possible that my actions set off a trap?" He gave me an inquisitive look.

"Of course."

"Great," he muttered. "Just great."

I felt my eyes closing as I watched him. I forced them open. We couldn't fall sleep here. As my mind drifted toward unconsciousness, I had an idea.

"Try ornaments."

"Ornaments?" A framed picture caught his eye and he walked over to it. I had an ominous feeling.

"The picture's crooked," Ven muttered to himself. He reached up to straighten it.

"Don't do that!" I was suddenly wide awake as I realized the danger in front of us. My warning came too late. He had already adjusted the frame.

Nothing happened.

I stopped for a moment, feeling confused. There might be a time delay, which would give us seconds to react. I grabbed his hand and pulled him to the door as an explosion rocked the room, throwing us against the wall of the passageway.

We lay on the ground for a moment with our bodies immobilized. My ears rang and my forehead stung from a cut.

"Ven?" I couldn't tell if I was shouting or not. He had been behind me and took the brunt of the explosion. "Ven?"

I heard a groan, and he sat up. "What was that?" He looked angry.

"It was a trap. They were designed to kill raider leaders. Only upper-class people would be concerned about a misaligned picture frame. They intended the explosion to take out people in command."

"That's disgusting. I need to learn how to leave a mess." Ven rose to his feet. I stood up too and peered back into the room.

"It is peculiar, but look."

We entered the room again. I was apprehensive about additional traps. I peeked into the hole made by the old-fashioned bomb. There was a second room behind the hole, inaccessible by any door.

"Let me guess. Is that the real guard's room?" Ven said looked at me for confirmation.

I nodded.

"Let's hope there's nothing dangerous in this one."

He was cautious enough to check things out before moving into the second room. When we were inside, we found a complete suite with a bed and a functioning bathroom.

I took off my shorts and tank top and crawled on the bed in my underwear. Ven fiddled with something near the hole we had accidentally blown in the wall.

"What are you doing?" I stretched out and curled up on the bed.

"Setting an alarm with a small force field, just in case. I came prepared, too."

"What will that do?"

"If anyone finds us, the force field will prevent them from entering and give them a mild shock. It will alert us to their presence."

"That's brilliant. I'm about to drop and can barely keep my eyes open."

He nodded and took off his suit jacket and button-up shirt. His pants came off next. Dust and dirt covered all our clothes. I swallowed as he climbed onto the bed next to me. It was just as hot in the catacombs as it was outside. We didn't need any covers.

"Keep your hands to yourself, mister." I gave another yawn.

"Of course. It's your move, anyway. I'm so tired that I'm ready for sleep. Seduction is the last thing on my mind."

"It's a good thing we have that settled." I tried to keep the sound of disappointment out of my voice. Wasn't he going to try anything? I rolled to my side away from Ven, already dropping off to unconsciousness.

A moment later, I felt Ven pull me against him, spooning me. His arm wrapped around my body, and I relaxed completely. I felt like I had to put up a minor protest.

"No sex."

"We're snuggling. There's a difference. I'm just keeping you safe." Those were the last words I heard before drifting off to sleep.

CHAPTER 19

VEN

My sleep felt thick, almost like someone had drugged me. As I swam up out of unconsciousness, my mind didn't want to wake up. I realized I was dreaming when I felt something soft pressing against me.

Keeping my eyes closed and moving instinctively, I began to explore. My hands felt an expanse of smooth skin. When they drifted up, I discovered soft mounds that begged me to squeeze them. I slid my hands under the fabric, the magnificent plump breasts responded to my touch, and I felt nipples begin to harden.

I molded and played with the flesh, enjoying a full breast in my hand. My cock was hard, and I pressed it against the female in my arms. Her butt felt round and juicy. All I needed to do was get these clothes out of the way, and I could fuck her from behind.

My balls ached for release, but I always made sure the woman was ready first. I slid my hand down her body until I found her sex. That was what I needed. I let my finger slip inside and found her dripping wet and so slippery that I would slide inside her without any problems.

What a sweet little dream.

My finger found the pleasure button that I knew would make her come and began to lightly stroke it. The woman finally woke up enough to moan, and I felt myself getting harder at the sound. I continued to rub her slick lips and play with the hard nub until she cried out and rocked back against me.

I realized that I had given Emmy an orgasm after promising I wouldn't touch her unless she asked me.

I took my hands away and turned my back to her. I would have blue balls from not being able to come, but it was better than being murdered in the morning. We hadn't had explicit sex. Right?

Something inside me knew my excuses wouldn't be enough this time. What was I thinking?

The truth was that I wasn't thinking. I had been half-asleep and horny. I felt like an asshole and hoped Emmy wouldn't hate me tomorrow.

* * *

EMMY

I didn't usually dream about sex, but I was having a good one right now.

There was a man in the dream. His hands were all over me, touching me everywhere, and it felt amazing. It didn't feel awkward when he put his hand down between my legs.

I thought I had died from pleasure. I had an amazing feeling that spread through my entire body, leaving me feeling weak and happy. But the dream wasn't enough. I needed more, wanting him to complete me. Then the man was gone, and I felt bereft. Where was he?

I moaned a sound of sadness, wiggling around. I felt his chest against my back. He was still there. I rolled to face him.

"Emmy." His deep voice sent shockwaves through me.

"I need more," I whispered to the dream man.

My hands roamed all over. His muscles were so sexy that I needed to kiss him. My bra was in the way. I pulled it off, removing my underwear and his in the process. That was better.

I found my way to his face, lying my nude body against him. He groaned and opened his mouth, our tongues twisting and mating in an erotic dance which made me wetter between my legs.

His arms wrapped around me and our bodies were pressed tight together. "Are you sure you want this, Emmy?" The sound of his voice triggered something and I came back to reality. Ven touched me. He made me come. He was right in front of me, and I wanted him to complete me.

"Yes, I'm sure." Was I begging? I felt like a wanton. "Please."

"I think you should come again. You need to be completely relaxed."

"I can do that again?" I gasped as he latched on to my breast, sucking hard.

He nearly made me come immediately from the exquisite touch of his mouth on my nipples. When his hand slid between my thighs and started rubbing my pussy again, my hips bucked involuntarily.

Ven flicked my clit until I was close, then he put a finger inside me. I moaned, loving the sensation. After a minute, when I was dripping wet, he slid in another finger. His fingers stretched me, and I gasped when he started pumping them in and out.

With his mouth on my nipples and his hand in my sex, I found myself coming again, even harder this time. As I lay silent, floating down from my high, I realized that Ven had disappeared.

"Ven?"

"I'm here." I turned my head and saw him open a tube, squeezing out a cream onto his fingers. "This will feel cold."

His skillful fingers materialized again, rubbing the cream inside me.

"What are you doing?" I felt my arousal building again.

"It will make fucking me less painful. It's a local anesthetic that will dull the pain, but let you feel all the pleasure."

"Someone thought he was going to get lucky," I murmured, feeling my hips bucking again from his ministrations. He put the cream away and lay down beside me. His eyes made me feel loved, and his gaze took my breath away. "Luck is a useful quality in a treasure hunter."

"I went to the store before leaving for the party." He moved the tube of cream aside. "There was a particular treasure I wanted to find."

"Were you so sure of your prize?"

"Nope. But I was hopeful."

He moved forward to kiss me, his mouth taking me, possessing me completely. I wanted him to do the same thing to my body. I had come twice already, but I still wanted and needed more. I felt empty and only he could fill me.

He kissed me for so long that I was wet and panting for him before he was ready to give me what I wanted. Finally, he kissed his way down my neck until he reached my breasts, making me shudder. Without warning, he took my aching nipple into his hot mouth. I arched up off the bed, moaning.

His hand dropped between my legs again. He slid his finger up and down my soaking wet lips, driving my desire higher.

"I need you. Now."

He was there in an instant. I felt him at my entrance, and I was scared and excited at the same time. He gazed into my eyes as he pushed in. I drew in a deep breath at the feeling of him inside me. He kept me pinned down and pushed in farther, making me writhe underneath his body.

"You feel fantastic, Emmy." He pushed in another inch. "Now." He thrust hard. I squeaked, but it didn't hurt. The cream was doing its job.

Soon he was deep inside my core, and our hips were pressed tightly together. He paused for a moment, letting me savor the feeling of being intimately close. I knew I would always want to be this close to him. I didn't know I wanted a man, but Ven had opened my eyes.

He pulled out and thrust inside again, causing a wave of pleasure to start building in my core. I lay on my back as he moved in and out of me. Soon I couldn't lie still any more and had to push back against him, matching him thrust for thrust.

"It's incredible," I moaned, feeling his movements taking me higher.

He leaned down and sucked one of my nipples into his mouth. That was enough to push me over the edge. My body exploded with sensation, shattering into a thousand pieces as I cried out in bliss. Contractions shook me, and I clung to Ven, who drove into me a few more times until his cock stiffened.

I felt his seed fill me. The sensation was so right that I shuddered with renewed ecstasy, milking every drop from him. Eventually, my convulsions stopped, and I lay still, totally satisfied, completely spent.

Ven was still on top of me, his weight pressing down on my body. I didn't care that it was hard to breathe. I was in heaven. He lifted himself onto his arms, keeping his cock in me, and dropped feather-light kisses all over my face. He was mumbling something over and over that was hard to understand.

It sounded like I love you.

CHAPTER 20

VEN

As I lay inside Emmy, I tried to piece myself together. I had good sex before but this was practically indescribable. Amazing? Mind-blowing? Unbelievable? The correct words didn't exist. I should have known things would be different with Emmy. She was unlike every other woman I had ever been with.

I wondered if my feelings could intensify the sensations of sex. Even though it was her first time, I hoped she thought it was special. I realized I felt something different. Did I love her?

The realization shocked me, but I knew it was true the moment it passed through my mind. I covered her face with kisses, whispering it over and over.

I loved this woman, and I would do anything for her.

* * *

We fell asleep twisted together. Her forehead was on my cheek. Neither of us spoke another word, not wanting to break the intimate spell of the night. I woke up hours later, feeling terrific. Emmy was already awake.

All I wanted to do with my morning erection was turn her around and fuck her again. But she might be sore. The cream had worn off by now.

The atmosphere seemed less romantic in the daytime, as well. We were in some catacombs, under a mountain on a foreign planet, racing to get a stupid ladle before someone else did.

I hoped she was right about this ladle, and it could heal people who were going to die. That was Emmy's reason for being here.

Another reason was more important to me. I looked down at my reason as her eyes locked with me. We stared at each other for a long time before Emmy averted her gaze and untangled herself from my body.

We took turns washing up and getting dressed in the bathroom. She didn't say said a word the entire time. As the silence stretched, I became afraid to say anything. Would she tell me it was terrible? Would she want to divorce me immediately because of a violation of the TerraMates agreement?

I might be able to raise an objection on that one. She begged me to make love to her, but I suppose there weren't any witnesses. I decided to stop being a coward when we were both dressed.

My voice sounded tentative, even to myself. "Emmy?"

"Ven, let's not ruin anything," she blurted out.

I walked over to her with fear in my heart. "Emmy." I lifted her chin, forcing her to look at me. "Last night was

183

fantastic. I've never experienced anything like what we had between us."

She nodded, looking relieved.

I paused. I didn't want to make her say anything if she wasn't ready, but I wanted to know if she was upset. I hoped she wouldn't say our relationship was over before it had a chance to begin.

"I don't know what to say or what to do." She trailed off, clenching her hands helplessly.

"You didn't...I mean, did you...enjoy it?" I had to ask. I had to know what it felt like for her. I was as careful as I could be. Everyone said a girl's first time wasn't her favorite sexual experience, and Emmy was a little girl from Earth.

"Oh, Ven." She turned away, her face bright red.

My heart dropped into my stomach, and I started babbling. "You didn't then? You know, they say the first time isn't going to be the best. Consider it a practice run. I'm sure you'll like it more the next time."

Shit.

"Shut up. I liked it, okay? Like isn't a strong enough word. I have never felt like that before, and I can't stop thinking about it, even though I'm not sure if we can do it again."

"What's the problem?" I asked, relief flooding my body.

"I don't know. Doesn't it make me a slut to have enjoyed it so much?"

"Emmy, women enjoy sex as much as men. It's part of the magic of being a couple. Sex is sometimes the glue that holds a relationship together or the band-aid that fixes things when you hurt each other. It's a way to connect on a deeper level with your partner. Don't talk about yourself that way or cheapen our time together."

I frowned, upset that she thought we had done something wrong when it felt right.

"Okay, okay. I'm sorry. I don't know what to do with myself today. We should go. With the amount of terrain we have to cover, we need to get moving."

"Agreed." Any conversations about our future together could wait until we knew we were going to have a future.

* * *

EMMY

After Ven had dismantled his alarm system, I led the way back into the passage. I walked gingerly because every step reminded me I had an ache between my thighs. I hadn't realized being sore could feel good. Every shift of my body was a painful reminder of everything we did last night.

I was still surprised at how good it felt. I hadn't expected sex to be like that. It has always seemed strange to me. But when I was in the midst of passion, everything was different.

I understood that now, but I didn't understand my feelings. I was happy, perhaps even blissful. My body still wanted him. Even though I knew fucking him wouldn't be pleasant until my sex healed, I hungered for him.

But I was confused.

Did he really whisper he loved me? I wondered if the words came from his heart or if it was the kind of thoughtless, stupid phrase that would come out of an Earth man's mouth after sex. I thought I didn't want a man or need a partner. Ven was making me question myself.

Did I love him? I had a plan for my life, and Ven wasn't part of it.

It might not matter if I was going to die here, in these passages, impaled on a spike.

We had traveled for about an hour before I spotted signs indicating a pan-jee trap in the floor ahead. Markings on the floor suggested danger, and when we stepped on them, we avoided springing the trap. We had evaded two more before we stopped for a break, sitting side by side on the stone floor, leaning against the wall.

Ven took my hand. It felt so nice that I didn't say anything.

* * *

VEN

"According to my calculations, we should be three-quarters of the way there by now. We're approaching the region of more sophisticated protections."

"You've got to be kidding me. What else is there?"

"Soon we're going to encounter an army of stone soldiers armed with functional, deadly crossbows. And there's supposed to be hematite powder. It's a metallic dust that's sharp on the molecular level and will cause a painful death if you inhale enough. Imagine having your lungs sliced to pieces."

She pulled two masks from a pocket in her pants and handed one to me. "If you see any white dust, put this on immediately, unless you want to die a slow death."

I took the mask and put it in my pocket. "Thanks. I prefer living."

We walked on in silence, each of us privately thinking until we came to a spot where the passage narrowed. At the end of the tunnel was an immense underground field covered in life-like statues.

"The stone soldiers." Emmy was barely breathing, and her eyes sparkled. "They're real."

As I stared at the evidence of the ingenuity of the ancients, I briefly understood Emmy's attraction to this field of study. I imagined what it would be like going to work and looking for the best of people instead of going to work to kill the worst of us all.

Everything about the ladle was like a big puzzle. I enjoyed looking for the signs indicating a trap was nearby. I liked trying to match wits with the people of the past. For a moment, I considered Emmy's suggestion about getting a degree in archeology, but it was a childish dream.

"How are we going to get across without dying?"

"I don't know, but it's even worse than you imagine. Do you see the wires crisscrossing everywhere? I'm sure they are all tripwires, and there are probably ones we can't see."

"We can't walk through there," I said. "We'll get ourselves killed. You're the smart one. Think outside the box. We won't win if we keep playing their games."

"What about the metal cable there?" She pointed up to the ceiling.

"It's probably left over from construction. If I had to guess, they used it to haul away dirt when they were excavating. You could throw another cable over the top, attach a container full of dirt and move it out of the room."

"That makes sense." Emmy was thinking. "It took them over a hundred years to complete these catacombs. It wasn't because of a lack of technology or tools, but because of funding."

"Of course. Was it a government project?"

She made a face at me. "They would have protected the cable to make it last. The legends say this room took nearly twenty years to build. They wouldn't have wanted it to deteriorate and endanger the workers. I think it's safe to say the cable can support some weight.

"So what?"

"It looks like we could slide down the line. On Earth, we have something called a zip line, where you attach a harness to a rope, then slide down."

Her intelligence intimidated me, but it could also lead to unique ideas.

"Stop looking at me like that," she said, frowning. "I'm being innovative."

"We don't call it a zip line on Stalwart, but I'm familiar with the concept. You're saying we could go over this obstacle, and skip their little game entirely. You have a point, but it sounds dangerous."

"Do you think it will be more dangerous than going through the stone soldiers?"

"We can't go through the stone soldiers, Emmy."

"That's my point. Even if the zip line approach is unorthodox, it might be our only way forward. It's brilliant, even if I do say so myself." She smiled and punched my arm.

"Don't hurt me. I have to slide down this rope in a minute." I pulled her into a hug. "If we're going to do this thing, let's not waste any time."

She nodded. "There's a ladder on either side allowing access to the cable."

"Wait a minute. The ladder hasn't been coated with chromate. It's made of wood." I was having second and third thoughts about her idea.

"That's true." She stood and looked up at the ladder. "But they did use darkwood to construct it, which is both insect and rot-resistant. There are still darkwood houses on Heralla from centuries ago. They look brand-new."

A short piece of rope appeared in her hands. She must have taken it from her bottomless pockets. She pulled out a knife and cut the rope in half, giving me a piece.

"Is the archeologist in you trying to tell me the ladder is safe?"

"No," she said. "I'm not saying that at all."

"I'm glad we agree on something. I'll go first."

"Why?"

"You've got all the necessary information. If one of us is going to plunge to their death, it should be me. I'm expendable. Also, I weigh more than you."

Emmy stepped forward and put her hand on the side of my face. "You're not expendable to me."

I smiled, and I kissed her, breaking it off before I became overwhelmed with the urge to take her.

"Don't worry, Professor. I'm not going to die today."

She nodded but looked more worried than before. I began to climb, testing my weight on each rung before trusting it. The first few feet seemed sturdy. I didn't look down. I was not afraid of heights, but I knew better than to risk distraction.

All I had to do was keep moving one arm after the other, and suddenly I had almost reached the top. After two more rungs, I would be able to use my rope and slide over certain death into a much safer probable death.

The rung broke, leaving me dangling by one arm forty feet in the air.

CHAPTER 21

EMMY

All I could think about was Ven swinging above my head, hangling by one arm, scrambling in a valiant attempt to grab hold of another rung to pull himself back onto the ladder. There was nothing I could do. It felt like the longest twenty seconds of my life. I had to stop looking.

His deep voice called down to me. "I'm okay." Perhaps he was all right, but I wasn't sure if my heart would ever be normal again. I was used to taking risks by myself and for myself. It was quite a different experience when I had to watch someone I cared for putting their life in danger.

Ven kept climbing and reached the top, flipping his rope over the cable with one hand, and keeping a firm grip on the ladder with the other. If the ladder collapsed before he secured himself on the wire, it would be the end of him.

My idea was stupid. If the cable had eroded over time, he would drop straight into the middle of the stone warriors. The number of things to worry about was endless.

He didn't know what I was thinking. "Be careful of the broken rung and make sure you test each one. They seemed to take my weight, but I don't know if I weakened them while I was testing."

"Okay. Be careful, Ven."

He nodded. "I'll see you on the other side." I knew he believed neither of us would die. But I also knew the odds were against us. We weren't the first people to look for the ladle. The simple truth was that no one ever returned. I didn't think it was necessary to inform Ven about that little bit of information.

Thinking about the future's problems didn't always help the present. Having to worry about another person made everything different. I wasn't usually this concerned about my survival. I had always assumed I would come back alive.

I watched with fear in my heart as he grabbed the rope with both hands. All he had to do was hold on. Gravity would do the rest. I pulled out a pair of gloves to strengthen my grip when it was my turn.

My body didn't move. I felt like I wouldn't be able to do anything until he was safe on the other side. He had his rope draped over the cable and held it with both hands. He took a deep breath, closed his eyes, then lifted his legs and began sliding down the line.

It was just as I imagined it in my head until something happened on the far side of the enormous cavern. I saw his body plummet to the ground. By that point, the drop wasn't too far, so the impact wouldn't hurt him too much. The problem was that he hadn't cleared the statues yet. He fell in the middle of a small group.

I heard the twang of a crossbow firing. Ven's cry of pain echoed across the cavern.

I grabbed onto the ladder and climbed as fast as I could. A poison-tipped arrow had just impaled the only man I ever cared about. We were far from medical attention, and I didn't carry an anti-venom kit around with me. If Ven was going to survive, his only hope was finding the ladle.

* * *

VEN

Everything started out fine as I glided across the top of the room. The problems started when I ran into an obstacle. A thick nest of insects had formed near the cable, creating an immovable barrier. When I ran into the nest, my motion completely stopped. I felt the abrupt change of speed in my arms. I involuntarily opened my hands and fell straight into the last group of statues.

I was able to roll when I landed, but I managed to trigger one of the crossbows, which still worked perfectly after all these years. Up close, the arrow looked like it was made yesterday. It cleanly sliced into my bicep and emerged on the other side of my arm.

My arm looked terrible, but I would live. With my working hand, I eased a multi-tool out of my pocket, activating the laser cutter and removing the arrowhead. That was the easy part. The hard part was pulling the arrow out of my flesh. I screamed in pain, but I only lost a small amount of blood. It appeared the arrow had missed hitting any major blood vessels.

I pulled the suit's handkerchief out from my breast pocket. It would be large enough to wrap around my arm. I managed to tie it with one hand and tighten the knot with the help of my teeth. After I had bandaged my arm and checked to make sure I wasn't leaking blood anywhere, I started to look around for a way out.

I couldn't see Emmy, but I knew she was on her way. I hoped she wouldn't fall too. She must have seen what happened to me and developed a plan to avoid the obstacle.

A moment later, I heard the sound of a rope sliding down the cable. I held my breath, waiting for her to hit the nest. If she fell, I wanted to be ready to get her out. When she got close to my position, she arched her back and swung her legs up. Her stomach muscles were functional as well as decorative. She wrapped her boots around the cable, using them to slow her descent until she slowed to a gentle stop.

Emmy wrapped her legs around the wire, letting go of the rope and grabbing the cable with her glove-protected hands. She hung from her hands and feet on the cable, and she began to inch down hand over hand. Emmy didn't stop until she reached a ladder. As soon as she climbed down, she went to my side.

"How do you feel?" she whispered.

I didn't know why she was whispering. We were the only people around. "I'm here," I whispered back. "Everything's still working."

"Did you get hit by an arrow?"

"I did, but it was a shallow wound. I already pulled it out. It wasn't a problem. See?"

She bit her lip, and her eyes looked scared. "They're probably not regular arrows. They're coated with strychnine."

As if on cue, the muscles in my legs started to spasm. Emmy's eyes looked so fearful than I wanted to comfort her but I couldn't move until the pain stopped.

"But if we can get you to the ladle, it should fix everything. Right?"

"Right." Relying on a mythical ladle that was supposed to cure anything wasn't my idea of a practical plan, but the poison was old. Maybe it would have lost its potency by now. It was still powerful enough to make my body ache.

"Do you think you can get up?" She peered at me through two statues that stood between me and a safe place.

"I can. But should I?"

She grimaced. "I don't know. I see at least two tripwires."

"What if I run as fast as I can and stay low to the ground?"

"You might have to. I don't know of any other choices. Let me trigger some of the tripwires before you start." Emmy left my line of sight for a moment and returned with a stick. She pushed the closest wires, making arrows fly out with familiar twangs before they landed harmlessly on the ground.

I looked at the floor and tried to plan out a course. The idea wasn't the best. I took a deep breath and began running.

It was hard to move fast when I was also trying to keep my body a small target. When I felt my foot hit a tripwire and heard the noise of an arrow, I dived to the ground and rolled, but I was too late. The bolt hit me directly in the chest, and it was a deep wound this time. I groaned but managed to crawl to Emmy. I only set off one more trap. The arrow flew harmlessly overhead.

"That was a terrible performance." She winced when she saw the arrow sticking out from my chest.

"I'm afraid you're going to have to pull it out," I said. "Every second will count if poison is involved."

Emmy moaned. "There's a reason I'm an archeologist and not a nurse."

"I hope you're a quick study." I felt my legs start to cramp up again. She took a firm grip on the arrow and pulled, but not hard enough. I felt the arrowhead tear my flesh. It wasn't out yet.

I groaned in pain. "You need to do a single pull with all your strength and remove it."

"I'm sorry!"

I felt her grab the arrow shaft again and hoped she could do it correctly this time. I needed her help. She yanked, the bolt came out, and blood started freely flowing. I had clenched my mouth shut, but a small moan still escaped.

She pulled out a flattened roll of gauze. I wondered what else she had in her pockets. A second later, she had my shirt off and began wrapping my chest. Once Emmy stopped the bleeding, she helped me put on my shirt again.

Pain seared through my chest and arm as I stood up stiffly. I tried to ignore both the pain and my stiffening legs. This place was not going to get the best of me.

"I'm fine. What's next?"

She turned to face a stone bridge, which stretched over a dark chasm. I didn't want to think about how far the fall might be. "We have to cross it." Emmy gestured to the stones laid in a swirling pattern.

"What are we waiting for?" I moved to walk across it.

Emmy put out her arm and blocked my path. "It's not that simple."

"Of course it's not."

"We have to figure out which stones are safe to walk on. If we step on the wrong ones, they fall away."

"Fine," I said, feeling impatient. "How do we determine the correct path?" The bridge. looked rectangular-shaped. Within the rectangle, stones were laid in a spiral.

"The stones have Karfalun markings on them. They're numbers. Each stone has a number from one to..." She fell silent and started counting. "It looks like thirteen."

"Do we step on them in counting order? That sounds simple enough."

"That sounds too easy. What do we know about spirals? They're pretty and an example of a vortex...they're also examples of the golden mean." She was thinking out loud. "The spiral is a mathematical construct."

"Aren't spirals more art than math?" I felt out of my depth again, but it didn't bother me.

She shook her head. "No, they're definitely math. I think they're based on the Fibonacci sequence from Earth."

Emmy didn't realize how attractive she became whenever she started discussing obscure mathematical concepts. She had opened my eyes, and it was getting more difficult for me to remember that I had avoided intelligent women in the past. The more time I spent with her, the more I realized that her brain was one of her sexiest attributes.

"Talk dirty to me, baby." I couldn't help flashing a grin.

She gave a startled laugh, and her eyes lit up. "You like that? Does it turn on the alien? How about this? A Fibonacci sequence is a series of numbers where you derive each number by adding the two previous numbers."

I fanned myself. "Come over here. If I'm going to die today, I want to hold you as much as possible before my time is up. I used to be intimidated by smart women, you know."

"Really?" Emmy looked like she found it hard to believe. "What changed?"

"I got to know you. Keep telling me about Fibonacci."

Emmy walked over to me and put her hands around my neck. I held her tightly as she explained how she thought about the puzzle. "The sequence starts at zero, so you add zero and one, and you get one, then you add one and one, and you get two. The beginning of the series is 0, 1, 2, 3, 5, and 8."

She pulled away. "I think that's how it goes. I wish we could test it and be sure. If we get something wrong, we're going to fall and die."

"We can try the first step without anything bad happening. If that one holds, we can do the next one. We just don't go on the same stones at the same time." I stopped talking when I noticed my voice trembling.

She studied my face. "Are you sure you're okay?"

"I'll be better when the poison is out of my body." I gave her a tight smile.

"Right. Let's get moving." Her face looked determined. "I'll step on the number one."

She put her foot onto the first tile and pushed down, keeping most of her body weight on solid ground as well as holding on to my hand.

"It seems safe enough." She transferred the rest of her weight onto the large square stone.

"Great. Which one's next?"

"Well, one plus one is two, so I should step on the number two stone."

"Sounds good to me." I wasn't paying complete attention to her plan. I thought she was smart enough to figure it out herself, and my head felt light. "Wait. Emmy, don't move."

It was too late. She had already pushed on the second tile. It fell away beneath her, and she stumbled into a gaping hole.

CHAPTER 22

VEN

By reflex I pulled on her hand with all my strength, yanking her back onto a sturdy tile.

She put her hand over her chest as if she was trying to contain the pounding of her heart. "Why didn't that work?"

"You forgot a number. If zero and one give you the first number, then the sequence begins with zero, one, and another one before you get to two."

She glanced at the hole where the two had been.

"Shit. You're right. 0, 1, 1, 2, 3. That's embarrassing. Maybe you should be the archeologist." She leaned over and kissed me on the cheek. "Don't believe anyone who says you're stupid."

I shrugged, my face burning. It felt like Emmy had given me permission to use intelligence I barely knew I possessed.

"Now what?" She turned to look at the spiral of stones.

"There has to be another number one."

Emmy examined the stones for only a second before she exclaimed in delight. "There it is." She pointed to her left side. "I didn't notice it before." She pushed on the stone and shifted some of her weight to it. "I think it is safe."

"That's a relief. You would have stepped on two if it was there but since it's not, the next number is..."

"Three, right?" She looked at me for confirmation, and I nodded.

"Okay." She tested it, transferred her weight and walked across the bridge. I followed a stone or two behind her.

"Five plus eight is... thirteen."

She looked at the gap. It was quite a distance. I knew I could jump it, but she had shorter legs than I did.

"We're almost there. Let's get off this damn bridge."

"The mistake made me nervous, Ven. We can't afford additional errors."

I didn't respond to her. I felt like I needed to get off the bridge and sit down. The world was spinning around me, and I thought I might pass out. In the meantime, Emmy moved to the back of her stone and leaped with all her strength. She missed her mark slightly, making the twelfth stone tumble away. Her chest landed on the secure rock and she pulled herself up and out of the way.

I couldn't afford to hesitate further and risk falling over the side of the bridge. I jumped and barely made it to the stone Emmy had just vacated. My body began to shake.

I didn't want to collapse in front of her, so I moved away and plopped my ass down on the floor.

"Everything okay?"

"I think I need to rest for a minute." I folded my arms over my chest, trying to prevent Emmy from seeing my spasming muscles. "What do we have to do next?"

"The final test forces you to confront your deepest fears."

"I'm not afraid of anything." In reality, the thought made me feel queasy. It was either my fear or the poison spreading throughout my body.

"That's because you have never had to face yourself. The Gate of Truth is supposed to be a lie detector. Not about what you say, but about who you are."

"That sounds confusing."

"The legends say only those who believe in their self-worth can pass. No one knows how it works, but somehow the sensors can measure whether you think about yourself."

She took my hand, and we walked up to a large arched doorway. She let go of me and immediately walked through. Nothing happened. She came out on the other side and smiled at me. "See? No problem."

"Wait a second. What happens if someone doesn't pass the test?"

She looked away from me. When the seconds stretched into a minute, I felt myself begin to sweat. "Just say it. We don't have a lot of time to waste."

"We don't know for sure. The stories aren't always accurate about everything." She swallowed.

"Any information is better than no information."

"Well, I might have heard a few stories about laser blasts turning would-be gate passers into ashes, but I'm sure you'll be fine." She didn't look sure.

Was my lack of self-confidence that apparent?

"Ven, do you remember how it felt when you worked out the Fibonacci sequence earlier?"

I smiled involuntarily.

"Try to remember that feeling. You succeeded in a challenging puzzle. Keep your successes at the front of your mind as you pass through. I believe in you."

I walked toward the gate and stared up at the strange symbols etched into the rock. Maybe Emmy was right. My mind filled with images of me overcoming obstacles. I remembered how effortless solving the Fibonacci sequence was, and I had done it better than Emmy.

When I reached the threshold, I paused, holding myself back.

"I don't think you're supposed to hesitate." Emmy glanced nervously up at the arch.

I closed my eyes and imagined how it felt for a fleeting moment to be my true self. I took a step forward through the arch and felt good.

Out of nowhere, my aunt's voice sliced into my consciousness.

What have you done, you stupid boy. You aren't ever going to amount to anything. Don't take another step.

For some reason, I stopped moving, and I couldn't start again. I heard Emmy shouting at me. She sounded like she was far away. "Keep going!" she called.

But I was frozen. I was an imposter and a sham. I couldn't go through the gate because I felt like I had lied my whole life. Emmy didn't know who I was. If she did, she would leave me. What was I thinking trying to go through a Gate of Truth? I was a pretender.

The telltale whine of lasers warming up filled the room. Emmy's voice called to me. "Ever since I met you, you've been amazing. You've taken care of me and risked your life when you didn't have to. But my thoughts are worthless right now. It only matters what you think about yourself." She paused. "I think I love you."

She sounded like she was crying. I closed my eyes, allowing the feeling of her love to fill my soul.

I took another step. I was intelligent and worthy. I could do anything. Emmy believed in me. The least thing I could do was believe in myself. The lasers retracted, and I knew I could make it past the gate.

Keeping my mind filled with positive thoughts, I walked into Emmy's waiting arms. She clutched me too tightly, but I wasn't going to complain. I was alive, and I knew who I was.

"I love you," she whispered into my chest.

I wanted to tell her I loved her too, but something felt wrong. I opened my mouth to speak when I was interrupted by another voice.

"I'm sorry to interrupt this happy reunion, but we've got a ladle on our shopping list. If you will excuse us, we're coming through."

Emmy pulled away from me. "Abel," she growled. "How the hell did you get here?"

"It was easy. I followed you." He had a smug smile on his face. "I even had a little help."

He stepped aside, and I saw Morley behind him, hands tied behind his back.

CHAPTER 23

EMMY

"You bastard." I was furious and ready to kill. "Let him go."

Abel just laughed. "Why would I do that? I might still need him. Hell, I might need you too. You've been a great help so far."

"You let us get away."

"That's right, Emmy. Don't forget, I brought you here. You didn't even need to find transportation yourself."

I snapped my mouth shut as I realized Abel had been controlling my actions every step of the way. "But how did you track us? I thought we scrambled your signal."

"You scrambled a signal, that's true." He looked thoughtful. "It required the use of some illegal technology, but it was all worth it in the end, don't you think?"

"Neurotracking? You bastard."

"I left one of my men with orders to try and stop you half-heartedly if you tried to escape. I wanted you to get away. I knew you wouldn't cooperate with me voluntarily. There was no way to make you tell me how to get here or force you to bring the ladle to me. I tried that with Morley before, and it didn't work."

I pressed my lips together, trying to hide how angry I was at myself.

"The solution was letting you think you were doing everything for yourself. That way, I could follow from behind, and you would never know."

"You lazy bastard. You wanted us to do all the work and waltz in after us to claim the ladle for yourself."

"No one was dancing. We lost four men to the statues before we noticed the ropes hanging overhead. It was an ingenious solution. I can see why Morley chose to work with you."

I couldn't believe I led this asshole right to Zelia's ladle. We wouldn't let him get it. Would we? I glanced at Morley, and he shook his head.

Unfortunately, Abel noticed our little exchange. "Don't play any games with me." His face looked terrifying. "You're going to take me all the way to the ladle. I'm going to drink from it and get healed."

Morley looked at Abel with a sad expression on his face. "That was always the goal."

"I doubt it. It's not like I would be able to use the ladle once it was in official hands. They would seal it, or set up a priority waiting list for humans and aliens from all over. I wouldn't have a chance."

"That's not true, Abel." Morley cut me off with a frown.

"Don't be naive, girl. To you people, it's just another bauble or cute artifact. It's the only thing that can save my life." He held up a skinny, shaking arm. "Look at this. I'm dying, in case you don't remember."

Morley looked at the ground. "I've always cared about you, Abel."

"I don't want to hear it, Morley. Let's go." One of his men poked Morley with a gun and he stepped forward, stumbling a bit.

Ven had been silent, absorbing the conversations around him. He whispered softly so only I could hear him. "The bridge."

That might work if I could trick them across. "Okay, then." I tried to look as upset as possible. "Let's go. You have to come through the Gate of Truth." I pointed to the archway, taking their attention away from the bridge.

Two of Abel's men immediately started forward and stepped on the wrong blocks, which fell away, dropping the men into the chasm.

Abel sighed. "You know they're not dead, Emmy. They have hover pads to stop their fall. They can't come all the way back up, but we can retrieve them later." Abel gave me a furious glance. His team now consisted of one woman and two men.

Three of them and three of us. The odds were almost even now, but Ven was out of commission, and Abel had the better of us. Secretly, I was relieved. I didn't want unnecessary deaths on my conscience.

"Tell us how to get across," he shouted.

I didn't say anything.

"Let's not make this difficult. Give me what I want, or I kill him, right now." He put his gun against Morley's head.

"I can't believe you're capable of this. Mother would be disappointed in you." Morley looked gray.

"Don't put me to the test. Do you want to know if I can murder my brother?"

The revelation stunned me. Was Abel Morley's brother? How come no one ever told me before? I looked to Morley for confirmation. He nodded, then dropped his eyes.

I didn't want to deal with dramatic revelations right now. Ven swayed beside me. I wondered if he looked paler than before or if I imagined it. His body seemed stiff, and he was sweating. Estimating the potency of centuries-old poison was difficult. With one arrow, I hoped he would have lasted a few hours, but two arrows had entered his body. He probably only had an hour before the onset of full-body convulsions.

"Tell them, Em," Ven muttered.

"Yes, tell us, Em." Abel couldn't prevent himself from mocking him.

It didn't matter if Abel came with us. The only thing that mattered was getting to the ladle and saving Ven's life.

"You have to step on the numbers in the correct order. The numbers which aren't part of the Fibonacci sequence will fall away."

"Clever." Abel muttered to himself and Morley winked at me. I was glad he was still alive, but I hoped we could keep him that way.

"So what's the correct path? Morley will be going first, so don't bother lying, unless you want to see him plummet to his doom."

"0, 1, 1, 2, 3, 5, 8, 13." I felt impatient as they crossed. "I'm interested in your plan to get through the Gate of Truth. Can you look in the mirror and consider yourself worthy?"

"It doesn't matter at this point. I'm going around the Gate of Truth. Let's call it Abel's Gate." Abel walked forward, pressing a small round device onto one of the columns.

Ven grabbing my hand and pulled me down. Everyone on the other side scattered, running as far away as they could. We realized Abel was prepared to use explosives. Ven fell on top of me. I couldn't see much, but I heard a loud blast. Debris fell onto our bodies.

"That human is not like you other humans," Ven whispered. When everything was quiet again, we stood up to inspect the damage.

"He's crazy. We can't be sure a structure thousands of years old will remain standing after destroying one of its primary supports. I don't think everything will come crashing down, but losing the Gate could destabilize this area. We should retrieve Morley and get away from Abel's team. Do you have any ideas?"

"Abel is desperate. He'll do anything to get the ladle, probably even kill."

I took Ven's hand and looked into his eyes. "Morley's alive for now. I want to keep it that way. We're not going to die either."

We saw everyone else start to get to their feet. Abel pushed Morley forward and over the rubble first.

We climbed the pile of rocks that used to be the Gate of Truth. Ven met Morley at the top, helping him climb down. Morley's hands were still tied behind his back. I was afraid he was going to trip and fall on his face.

"Leave him alone. No tricks, Emmy." Abel waved his blaster in our direction.

"I'm trying to help him down," Ven said. "You've tied his hands. It makes it hard for anyone to move."

"Fine." Abel gestured with his blaster. "Move away from him now. We'll move his hands in front of his body so he can move."

Abel made a sharp motion, and one of his team came to bind Morley's hands. "Let's go," Abel called.

I glanced at Ven as we moved down the open passageway. Sweat had started dripping off his face, and his breathing was erratic. He needed to use the ladle soon.

After a few minutes of walking, we came to a closed door. I turned to look at Morley questioningly, and he nodded. We were at the finish line.

We had done all the research. It was hard work collecting information on the myths and legends surrounding Zelia's ladle. The only thing we had no information about was the final test.

Everything we learned about the ladle was shrouded in mystery, but the last obstacle was a total enigma. As far as we could tell, there were no stories about it. All we heard were frustratingly vague rumors.

We walked into a strangely-shaped room. To our surprise, the Silver Mestolo of Zelia was inside. It rested at the far end of the room on an altar. It wasn't even in a case.

Maybe the reason why we never heard anything about a final test was that there wasn't one.

The ladle had a silver hue because of its composition. It was made from filaden, an unnatural element with a high concentration of Higgs boson particles. The ladle was encrusted with yellow jewels. The gemstones were vital for preserving the stability of the metal.

It was amazing to discover the ladle was real, but as my sense of wonder faded, I started to look around the bizarre room. The surroundings were long and narrow — perhaps twenty feet across. At both ends, the floor sloped upward. From the outside, it looked like the letter U.

Alcoves were cut out of the rock walls every few feet. Each one was waist-high. Inside were small pools with beautiful golden fountains in the shape of Heralla deities. The water sparkled and the sounds soothed my mind.

The others caught up with us. Abel let out a strangled cry.

"It's finally within my grasp," he whispered to himself. Abel rushed across the room. "You won't stop me this time."

"Do you honestly think no further safety precautions are surrounding the ladle? You may be a fool, but I didn't know you were stupid."

Abel paused momentarily.

"Do you remember the stone soldiers?" Morley was getting louder. "If they took the time to build those statues, why would they leave the ladle lying around for anyone to take?"

"Figure it out. You're supposed to be the smart one. How do we get it? And you better hurry up," Abel said, nodding his head at Ven. "He looks like he could use the ladle right now."

I turned my head to look at Ven. As his legs spasmed, he lost his balance and collapsed on his ass. The poison had started to consume his body already.

"You're going to have to untie Morley," I said, deciding to give Abel a few orders. "If you want that ladle you'll do as I say."

I stared at Abel angrily, exhibiting a power I didn't know I had. Ven wasn't going to die if I could do anything about it. He tried to hold my gaze but quickly surrendered, giving a nod to someone who cut Morley's bonds.

"What's wrong with Ven?" Morley asked.

"He got hit with two arrows."

"You know they're coated with strychnine, right?"

"Of course I know." I cut him off. "This ladle better work or death will be his reward for helping me find it."

"How much longer does he have?"

"I think he'll be in real trouble in about twenty minutes."

Behind me, Ven's body was starting to convulse. I felt tears welling up in my eyes, but I blinked them away. "Let's just take it. I don't care who ends up with it at the end as long I can use it now."

CHAPTER 24

EMMY

I ran and checked Ven's pulse. It was erratic, but it existed. I stood up and made my way back to Morley, trying to hide my terror.

Morley knew me too well. He could sense my feelings with a look. "You care about him, don't you?"

I nodded, unable to speak.

"Let's do what we have to do. Zelia's ladle appears to be on the altar, ready for the taking."

"It can't be that easy. If we try to walk up and take it, something's going to try to kill us." I didn't want to make another mistake.

"I agree." Morley rubbed his chin thoughtfully.

"Don't you think the monks were using the ladle at the same time they guarded it? They were supposed to live for a long time and be almost impossible to kill. If the legends are true, it would make sense for them to be regularly drinking from the ladle."

"Right. They would need a way to get to the ladle without killing themselves." We walked gingerly into the room and looked around, examining the floor and walls but avoiding the area that contained the ladle.

"There's one fact on which everyone agrees. The stories all say the Stone Goddess will destroy anyone who tries to touch the ladle."

"The Stone Goddess." Morley looked up at the ceiling. "Do you remember the dig we did on Tyrranus 4? There was a giant rock that fell at the end and almost killed everyone on the team. If the mechanism hadn't rotted away, we might not be standing here today." He looked at me expectantly.

I snapped my fingers. "The Stone Goddess is always represented as a stone wheel with the outline of a woman over it. If the wheel is an actual thing, it would be perfect for smashing intruders to smithereens."

"Exactly." Morley nodded. "Look at the design of the room. The wheel will fall and start rolling, crushing everything in its path. When it reaches the end, it will roll up as high as it can. Gravity will pull it back down into the room and crush anything it missed. The wheel will move back and forth like a deadly pendulum until it pulverizes everything in its path."

"It could be set in motion if anyone touches the ladle." I felt the familiar excitement which came from solving the riddles of the ancients. "What if there is a scale or weighing mechanism built into the altar? They wouldn't need any further protections."

"Why would anyone risk destroying the thing they wanted to protect?" Abel had moved behind us and had a skeptical look on his face.

Morley didn't stop looking but still took the time to answer. "A giant stone that crashed onto the ladle wouldn't crush it. It's essentially indestructible."

Abel didn't say anything else. I supposed he was satisfied with Morley's response. Thinking about Morley's words, I remembered the inscription on the stone wheel at the festival.

"At City Hall, for the Festival of the Stone Goddess, there was a wheel with an inscription. It said, 'The Stone Goddess leaves no survivors'."

There was a hairline crack in the ceiling shaped like a rectangle. "There it is. Do we trigger it or try to avoid it?" Sometimes it was necessary to activate traps in a controlled way that prevented anyone from getting hurt.

"I think we should try to avoid this one." Morley thought for a moment. "What does it mean if she doesn't leave survivors? The extent of the danger isn't clear. It seems like someone would survive a wheel rolling around. There must be something less obvious."

"Be careful, Morley." He nodded and approached the altar at a crawl. It took an agonizing five minutes for him to advance ten feet. He always checked everything imaginable. His meticulous nature and his intuition were the only reasons he was still alive. After studying the ladle and the altar, he nodded. "It's a weight trap. You can tell by these signs..."

"I don't think we have time for extensive explanations."

"Right. Abel, do you have anything that can weigh the ladle without disturbing it?"

Abel nodded his head. A woman on his team pulled out a device and aimed it at the ladle, calling out the weight.

"We think the object itself is the tripwire. We need to swap it out with something with approximately the same weight. It's a classic protection because it's effective." Abel's team was already busy weighing rocks and various objects they carried.

"This device is close, but it's a little heavier." The woman handed a piece of gear to Morley.

"Don't give it to me yet. Remove parts or cut off plastic until the weight comes down. We need to make sure the weights are as close as possible." With a sigh, she took out her knife and began scraping off some of the plastic.

"Making the swap is going to be tricky." Morley looked nervous. Tricky was an understatement. Abel eagerly began to approach the altar but we both ignored him. He wasn't close enough to disturb us.

Slowly, Morley set the device down next to the ladle. I stood on the other side, waiting for the right time. When we were both ready, I started sliding the device toward the ladle while he pulled the ladle away.

At the back of my mind, I vaguely realized Abel was suddenly directly behind Morley, but I was concentrating on moving the things in front of me a little bit at a time.

Morley finally retrieved the ladle from its resting place as I simultaneously slid my weight into position.

As soon as Morley pulled the ladle away, Abel bumped him, reaching for the prize. After waiting for so many years, he couldn't last a second longer. Abel's greed triggered a series of events. Abel inadvertently pushed Morley's hand into the weight, moving it from the correct position. I quickly pushed it back, but it was too late.

Morley and I looked up. We heard the grinding of old gears and stone against stone. I glanced at Morley. Usually, he was calm even in the most difficult circumstances, but I knew he was genuinely afraid this time. We heard the sound of something large moving inside the ceiling.

Abel wasn't paying attention to any of it. He stared desperately at the ladle, clutching it tightly in his hands as he ran to the closest fountain.

Morley and I moved together. We each picked up one of Ven's arms, lifting and dragging him from the room. Abel's team had already disappeared. Ven had a massive body, and my half was hard to carry.

He groaned but didn't wake up. When we were almost to the door, I made a decision and released him.

"Morley, there's no point in getting Ven out of here if we have to leave the ladle behind. I'm going back to get it."

"You're going to take it from Abel by yourself?" Morley asked. "He's going to kill you. Even if he doesn't, the stone wheel will crush you."

It felt like the room was listening to our conversation. We heard the sound of something massive rolling around in the ceiling.

"I have to get the ladle." I was prepared to do anything to get what I wanted. "Even if we can move Ven out of here, we won't be able to save him without it."

I ran back to where Abel stood by the fountain, carefully dipping the ladle into the water. I held my breath, walking up behind him. Would I be able to grab it and go?

He took a deep breath and drank.

The rumbling noises that sounded so far away were getting louder. Less than a minute had passed since Abel inadvertently activated the trap, and I knew the Stone Goddess's wheel was coming to smash us all into tiny pieces. I dived for the ladle as soon as he finished drinking, but misjudged the distance and missed badly.

Abel moved back. "You're never getting it." His eyes were full of hatred.

"Please." Despair threatened to take over my soul. "I'll give it back. My friend needs it, just like you."

"He's nothing like me. For one thing, I've already used the ladle."

The noise in the background grew so loud that it overwhelmed our conversation. I couldn't hear the rest of his words. The stone wheel materialized overhead, showering red dust over our bodies as the ceiling shattered.

Abel and I both started running for the door, but it was too late for us. A piece of rock slid into place, covering the door and sealing the room.

If there had been any question about the strange shape of the chamber, it was definitively answered as the wheel crashed onto the altar, destroying it. The stone began rolling to us, gradually picking up speed.

The inscription was right. Was it possible for us to survive?

CHAPTER 25

EMMY

The huge wheel of the Stone Goddess was going to crush us. We had nowhere to run.

Abel was pissed. "I can't believe it." His face looked miserable. "I just got healed, and I'm going to die under a rock."

An idea popped into my head. "Let's go into one of the fountains." Before I darted away, I stole the ladle out of his hands.

"You're not taking that from me." Abel started running after me. The wheel was forgotten for a moment while he concentrated on retrieving the ladle. But I had it now, and I wasn't giving it up until I saved Ven.

The fountains were set into the tunnel walls. If we managed to stuff ourselves inside, the wheel would roll by and completely miss us. I climbed into the nearest fountain, not caring if I got drenched. I fit inside perfectly if I pulled my legs to my chest. I squeezed against the far side as the enormous wheel rumbled past.

The wheel rolled up as far as its momentum would take it, then reversed and began to retrace its path, picking up speed again and spinning by me. I glanced down at my arms. They were covered in white dust from the ceiling.

Now that I wasn't facing imminent death, I began to form a plan to get the ladle, fill it with healing water, and bring it to Ven. The first step was securing the ladle. I unbuttoned my shirt and tucked it inside, buttoning my clothes over the artifact. I checked to make sure my shirt was tightly tucked in and shifted my thoughts to getting out of the room.

The door wouldn't work any longer, but I was sure there was another way out. We thought monks had used the ladle in the past. If they did, they would need an escape route in case someone accidentally triggered the wheel of death.

Where was the emergency door?

The fountains were the first place anyone would go to escape the wheel. I held my breath as it rumbled past me again. Its weight and destructive force were frightening even though I was safe for now.

If the fountains were a natural hiding place, any escape door was probably located inside. I turned slightly and examined the outer wall of my fountain, looking for anything indicating a door. I pressed everything I could see and ran my hand over the surface of the walls and floor. Nothing happened.

What if I was in the wrong place? Did I have to check all the other fountains until I found the one with a door? What if my guess was incorrect, and I was looking for something that didn't even exist? I closed my eyes. I decided to check all of the fountains on my side first, then cross over and investigate the other side. I didn't know how long the big rock would keep its momentum, but I guessed it could continue moving for some time.

As the stone wheel rolled past me again on its way to the other side of the room, I jumped out of the fountain, ran as quickly as I could, and dove into the next fountain.

After examining it, I realized there wasn't a door in this location. Two fountains later, I sat back to catch my breath and looked across the room. Something caught my eye in the fountain directly across from me.

A deity inhabited each fountain. The one across from me held a representation of the Stone Goddess. My heart sped up. Was that the fountain with the door? It would make sense to indicate which fountain had the escape route. The Stone Goddess kills, but the Stone Goddess also saves. There was a poetic symmetry somewhere.

I prepared myself and waited. As the stone wheel rolled past again, I dashed across the room and scrambled up into the fountain of the Stone Goddess. I made it with only a second to spare as the rock rumbled past me once more.

A moment later, I was examining the alcove, searching for a mechanism to open a secret door. I pressed everything imaginable, but I found nothing.

Did Ven have much more time? What if he was already dead? When Morley and I lifted him, Ven had groaned, so he was alive at the time. I clung to the hope that I could find Ven with time to spare, but that would only be true if I got out of here.

My arms were still covered in white dust. Was something the matter with white dust? It was dangerous, but I carried a cure with me.

I took the ladle out of my shirt and grabbed onto the Stone Goddess's hand, using her to hold steady as I reached into the water and filled the ladle.

I took a sip, relishing in the cold drink. As I refreshed myself, a previously-unseen door swung open by itself, revealing a dark passageway. Either pressing on the hand of the Goddess opened the door or taking a drink did.

Before I left, I was going to take some magic water with me. I carefully filled the ladle again, then moved awkwardly around the fountain into the dark passageway. A giant insect dropped down in front of me, and I batted it away. Shuddering, I stood up in the passage.

I was comfortable with man-made obstacles, but I didn't like any biological threats. It was dark in the tunnel, and it was difficult for me to see. I hoped I wouldn't run into anything terrible.

After a few minutes of clumsily shuffling through the darkness, I bumped into a door and spilled some of the precious water.

"Fuck." I felt around, being careful not to drop any more. I didn't know if the amount of water was crucial but it might be the difference between life and death for Ven.

The door swung open, revealing so much light that I started to blink. I moved slowly out the door being careful not to empty the ladle. When my eyes had adjusted to the brightness, I saw Morley with his back to me, kneeling next to Ven. Ven was unconscious on the floor.

I strode ahead, keeping my eyes focused on the ladle. As I approached, Morley heard my footsteps and turned around. "My girl, I thought I lost you." There were tears in his eyes.

"I'm tough to kill." I smiled when I saw he was alive. "I brought the ladle, and it's full of water."

"Ven needs it right away. He stopped breathing."

I knelt down beside Ven. His body looked as solid as a board, and he was clenching his muscles. Morley was on his other side and opened Ven's mouth.

"Do you think I should just pour it in?"

Morley nodded, his eyes shining. He had waited twenty-five years for this moment.

I placed the ladle against Ven's lips and tried to keep my hands from shaking. I tipped it carefully until all the water dribbled into his mouth. After that, all we could do was wait.

After a minute had passed, there was no sign of movement. My tiny flicker of hope turned into despair.

"This stupid ladle's not doing anything." I felt a lump in my throat. Everything we sacrificed had been in vain. Ven was going to die today. I couldn't stand it.

"Be patient." Morley was trying to be kind, but I could see he was losing hope. The years spent searching had been a fool's errand. We had risked our lives for an illusion.

I closed my eyes, pressing my fingers against his neck, tears spilling out as I frantically checked for a pulse. Nothing. He had no heartbeat.

Ven was gone.

CHAPTER 26

VEN

I drifted in and out of consciousness, floating outside of my body. There were voices. One belonged to a woman, and others blended into a cacophony. I remembered I was supposed to do something, but I wasn't sure what it was. The thought was on the outskirts of my mind. It vanished every time I tried to focus on it.

The woman was someone important. We were doing something together. I didn't know what.

What I did know was that pain filled my body. Agony was a part of every muscle, bone, and nerve. The last thing I wanted to do was think about my suffering. I noticed a beautiful light. It was peaceful and beckoned to me. I knew if I went into the light all my pain would go away.

Merely moving in the direction of the glowing light felt wonderful. I sighed, feeling my pain start to disappear. I was about to enter the light when I paused.

Wasn't there something I was supposed to do? It was related to the woman. Was she important?

The light had a magnetic pull on me, and involuntarily I began moving to it again. I heard a noise in the distance and imagined my body was moving, but everything seemed far away. The light was right here. I felt torn in two directions. It was time to enter the light, but a little

231

part of me was reluctant to surrender. Could I stay and bear the pain?

I don't know how long I floated between the light and the pain. The place was timeless. I wasn't in a hurry. I had to choose between doing something easy and doing what was necessary.

Without warning, the pain receded. I felt an intense relief and immediately moved back toward my body. I glanced longingly at the light, but I realized I wasn't supposed to be there yet. I had things to do. I felt like I had been underwater and was going back up for a breath of air when my consciousness reintegrated with my body.

Crashing back into reality, I woke up.

* * *

Everything hurt. I could hear the sound of someone crying. My eyelids were so dry that I could barely pry them open. When I finally managed to open my eyes, I wasn't sure where I was.

It was bright here too, even though I had turned away from the light. A woman's head was on my chest. She was sobbing like she had a broken heart. I vaguely recalled someone crying like that on my shoulder before. I wondered why it didn't make me uncomfortable.

Suddenly I remembered everything. Searching for the ladle, making love to Emmy, getting hit with poisoned arrows, and passing out. I had no idea what had happened after I lost consciousness. All I knew was that

Emmy was crying on my chest like she had lost a family pet.

I tried to speak, but the only thing that came out of my mouth was a croak. Her head came up, and I tried again. "What's wrong, Emmy?" I thought I managed to speak clearly this time. She started weeping even louder than before, and Morley appeared from somewhere. They both talked at the same time. I wasn't sure what they were saying. My brain felt a bit fuzzy. I knew I had to tell her one thing before I thought about doing anything else.

"Listen to me." My voice was rough, but it worked. She took my face in her hands and gazed into my eyes.

"I love you." Now she knew, and I could die in peace. She closed her eyes as if she were praying and leaned down to kiss me soundly on the lips.

Her touch made me feel much better. Maybe it wasn't the kiss. I felt like I was regaining strength with each passing moment. The pain and stiffness were receding in my limbs. Soon I felt strong enough to sit up.

Morley and Emmy exchanged incredulous glances. I shook out my arms, which seemed to be working. I wiggled my legs. Did the poison leave my body? I pulled up my shirt to check on the wound on my chest and saw a round, pink scar.

"I guess the ladle is real. It worked."

Emmy nodded and hugged me. "What about Abel?" she asked. "He's still in there."

Morley nodded and walked down the hall, going through a small door. He was back a few minutes later with Abel in tow.

"You didn't even tie him up?"

"He's my brother, Emmy."

"Not to me. He's a danger to everyone." She shook her head.

Before they could enter into an argument, the room started to shake. Dust began falling from the cracks in the ceiling.

Morley looked at Emmy in dismay. "Taking the ladle was the last straw."

"Are you saying there's additional danger?" Abel looked incredulous.

Morley shook his head. "We have to get out of here. It sounds like the entire catacombs are at risk."

"The Stone Goddess leaves no survivors," Emmy whispered to herself.

Cracks appeared in the ceiling and the walls. Dust poured out of the cracks, coming down in a thick cloud that threatened to cover us.

Emmy started shouting above the noise. "It's not regular dust. It's hematite. Put your mask on!"

She was already wearing her mask. My hand reached into my pocket and pulled out the cover, putting it over my face. Morley produced a mask for himself, and Abel was forced to cover his nose and mouth with his shirt.

Morley motioned to the tunnel, and we followed him quickly. Once inside, we saw two paths go in different directions. One appeared to lead back to the ladle's resting place while the other had stairs leading up. "We have to climb. I'm not sure how much time remains."

I moved behind Emmy, and we raced up the stairs together. I kept looking back to confirm Morley was still behind us. I didn't care if Abel died down here, but I was determined to make sure Morley came with us.

In case we needed further incentives, dust and stones began to fall in the stairwell. Emmy slipped, but I caught her ass. We stayed on our feet. My muscles started to ache from the effort, and my lungs were burning. I hoped my breathing problems were from the exertion, and not because I accidentally inhaled hematite.

We had started to slow down when we came to a door. More rocks were filling the stairwell. One crashed into my head. When I touched my forehead, my fingers came away wet with blood.

Emmy was fumbling with the door. There was a handle, but I could see her searching for a puzzle. Morley pushed past her and leaned on the release. "Sometimes things aren't complicated."

We all slipped out of the door, emerging onto the mountainside where we saw Abel's team trudging down the mountain. It was cold in the shadow of the cave, and we moved out into the blissful heat of the two suns. Looking through the door, we could see the demise of the structure. I held Emmy's hand as the catacombs which kept the Silver Mestolo of Zelia safe for centuries collapsed into ruins.

CHAPTER 27

EMMY

I leaned into Ven's side, putting my arm around his waist. He smelled wonderful. I couldn't wait to take him home. It was our one-year wedding anniversary today, and I was going to give him a gift he would remember for a long time. The new lingerie I was wearing was only the first part.

Distracted by Ven's delicious scent, I had missed whatever Morley was talking about. We were part of a small crowd of archeologists in a beautiful new building. Morley was making a speech and would soon cut a ribbon opening the Morley Davidson Wellness Center featuring the Silver Mestolo of Zelia. Modern technologically-based security heavily guarded the ladle. No more rolling stone wheels.

The plan was for the center to treat terminally ill patients who were incurable. People could take a drink from the ladle, then get educated on how to keep themselves healthy. A wellness center had been Morley's dream since he first learned about the ladle. From the time he started on the adventure to heal his brother, he had focused on this goal.

Surprisingly, Abel was at his side. He was shocked by his near-death experience and went through a change of heart. He apologized and asked for Morley's forgiveness. Reconciling with his brother made Morley happier than I had ever seen him before. He loved his brother and was deeply hurt by their schism.

I was happy for my mentor and planned on working with him for a long time. We had all taken a drink from the ladle, of course. We expected the single drink to increase our life span by thirty years.

Ven had found a purpose in his life. He decided to go back to school and was taking courses in archeology. He had discovered a new interest. Once he graduated, we would work side-by-side, hunting down artifacts and learning from the wisdom of the ancients.

In the ceremony, Morley was cutting the ribbon. Ven squeezed my hand, and we smiled at each other, briefly releasing our hands so we could clap. He leaned down to whisper in my ear. "I can't wait to get you home." His breath sent tingles down to my core.

"Oh?" I tried to play innocent. "Why would that be?"

"I know what you're wearing under your dress."

I blushed and bit my lip, trying not to smile. "I have a present for you." I gave him a coy look.

"As long as it's not something dusty and old, I'll take it. I've had enough of that to last a lifetime." He grinned at me.

"I wouldn't give you an ancient artifact for our anniversary. This gift is much wetter and is definitely alive."

His eyes darkened, and I drew in a breath at the sight of his desire.

"I'll search for that treasure any day, my love." He gave me an intense look that set my core on fire. We made our way to congratulate Morley. Now that the ceremony was over, we were ready to go home. Neither of us could wait to celebrate our first year of marriage.

* * *

We hurried home, both of us on edge. As soon as we entered the bedroom, he pushed me up against the door and started kissing all over my body. Soon we were both so wound up that we couldn't wait another minute. He quickly stripped off my dress and made quick work of his clothes.

He paused for a moment when he saw my bright red lingerie. It was a red satin bra and matching panties. "Those look fantastic, but right now, they've got to go."

I didn't care as long as he fucked me immediately. I could wear them another time. In fact, I didn't have to wait for him to undress me. He was naked already, and I pushed him onto his back on the bed. His eyebrows flicked up. I usually let him take the lead, but not this time. I needed him. I was going to take what I wanted.

He moved back until he was against the headboard. He watched me slowly undo the clasp of my bra and pull it off. I heard his breath catch when my breasts came into view. Then I slid out of my panties and dropped them on the floor, crawling over to him, ready to take him and make him mine.

I had already soaked my underwear, so I knew I was ready. I positioned myself over him and slowly took his cock into my body. He filled me, and I closed my eyes in ecstasy at the sensation of being penetrated deep inside my core. I sank completely, covering the last inch of his cock and making our pelvises flush.

I couldn't speak. I felt my orgasm building already, and I had barely moved. I raised myself up and let him push back inside. It felt amazing. I rode up and down on him, increasing my pleasure. He rubbed against my G-spot in a way that drove me crazy.

"That's good, Emmy. Ride me." Ven moved his hands to my hips. He leaned forward and took one of my nipples into his hot mouth. I gasped at the feeling and started to rock faster. He sucked hard, then switched to the other side. That was enough.

I came hard, moaning and contracting around him. He held my hips still and drove up into me several times before he stiffened and emptied himself into me. I wrapped my arms around him and held on as shudders wracked my body. The bliss continued until I finally stopped moving and collapsed with my head on his shoulder, feeling spent.

After a while, he whispered to me. "You're my treasure, and I'm glad I found you. I love you."

"I love you, too." I had a lazy grin on my face. He said kissed me until I forgot treasure hunting, archeology, and everything except for him.

"Now that you've found me, what are you going to do with me?" I gazed into his eyes.

"I'm going to hold onto you and never let you go."

If you enjoyed this book, please review it on Amazon! Your review helps me succeed as an author.

To stay up-to-date on my latest releases, sign up for my newsletter at:

http://lisalace.com/newsletter/

OTHER BOOKS BY LISA LACE

WATER WORLD WARRIOR: A TerraMates Novel

Why would I want to be married to an alien?

I should not have applied to TerraMates! The idea was crazy. I'm a young woman, in the prime of my life.

But I was desperate.

When I landed on another world, his appearance intrigued me. He dripped sexuality and moved like an animal. We have three days together before he sets sail without me. Am I going to escape or submit to my desires?

TAKEN: A TerraMates Novel

What happens when TerraMates runs out of applicants?

There's never a shortage of wealthy alien bachelors looking for the thrill of mating with a human. They want our women.

But despite the promise of riches, sometimes the pool of available brides runs dry.

How does TerraMates find more girls, and where do they go? When Lyzette gets taken off the street, she finds out.

WATER WORLD CONFIDENTIAL: A TERRAMATES NOVEL

He needed a wife. I wanted an alien lover.

The first time I saw Jori, I hated everything about him. He didn't care about anything except himself. On the other hand, his body was spectacular, and his muscles were firm. I couldn't stop thinking about him.

When TerraMates gave me the chance to marry Jori, I took it. I knew I needed the money. What I didn't know was that Jori's exterior was a facade, and he had kept secrets from everyone his entire life.

ALPHA'S ENSLAVED BRIDE: A TERRAMATES NOVEL

Knowing the future isn't a blessing. It's a curse. Especially when you've seen your death.

I'm going to die in the arms of someone I have never seen before. He's a person I will love, but I don't know anything about him.

When TerraMates matched me with Airik, I couldn't believe it. This sexy alien could see the future, just like me. I wasn't alone anymore. I quickly found out he knows nothing about Earth or humans. I married him, but will I be safe with him?

AUCTIONED TO THE ALPHA: A TERRAMATES NOVEL

The innovative TerraMates business has been a runaway success. Who wouldn't want to marry an alien?

Seeking to expand, TerraMates has opened new locations with different business models.

Eden is looking for a fresh start and is one of the first mail-order brides from New York City. As soon as she signs the paperwork and collects her credits, she blacks out.

When Eden wakes up, she's been married to an alien bounty hunter. She's ready for a new beginning, but all she knows about her alien husband is that he's handsome and dangerous. Eden never dreamed she'd be chasing criminals through space!

WRONG ALIEN: A TERRAMATES NOVEL

Life isn't worth living without an Internet connection. I'm always on the computer, video chatting, and even reading books on my phone.

It was natural for me to use the TerraMates app to find a husband.

I didn't know they would match me with a sexy alien who was afraid of high technology and send me to a mysterious planet where the penalty for having a smartphone was execution!

NAIMA: A TERRAMATES NOVEL

I never thought I'd find my soulmate through a mail-order bride agency. I never thought he'd be an alien warrior.

He calls me naima. His beloved.

When I'm on my way to meet him face-to-face, my shuttle is attacked, and we crash onto a planet in the middle of a war. I didn't sign up to be an alien comfort woman. I need my naima to rescue me.

www.ingramcontent.com/pod-product-compliance
Lightning Source LLC
Chambersburg PA
CBHW020602180626
46810CB00007B/2607